# THE SEASONS OF HEARTBREAKS

# THE SEASONS OF HEARTBREAKS

**NATASHA LAKSHMI**

ISBN 978-1-4477-4301-9

FOR, MY COUSIN YASHO & GRAHAM HUFF.

# Chapter One
## <u>40 Year Old Cathy</u>

San Francisco an upbeat and beautiful modern city of America. A 40-year-old woman was in the colourful and happy city, but she didn't want to spread the colours of joy in her life. Someone was going to do that for her.

But how long could Cathy wait for that to happen?

Cathy a black eyed woman with shoulder length blonde hair was wearing black trousers, black high heel shoes with a white shirt on, was carrying her black handbag on her right shoulder, she was holding a medium size blue plastic box which was light that had 15 exercise books in, as she was walking in the street she looked like a dull boring person, she hardly smiled or laugh she looked serious. Cathy couldn't walk any longer in the street and her hands and arms were tired of holding the plastic box, she sees a taxi parked near by the side of the road, it was a bold fat man who was the driver sat there waiting for a passenger, she goes up to the taxi and she opens the car door with her left hand, holding onto the plastic box in with her right hand and she gets in the car and she shuts the door.

Cathy tells the taxi driver to take her to Nob Hill where she lives.

Cathy lives in a 3-bedroom house with her parents. You would think at her age she would be living on her own,

BUT FOR HER SHE DIDN'T WANT TO BE ON HER OWN, SHE DIDN'T
HAVE ANY FRIENDS TO HAVE FUN OR PARTY WITH.

CATHY'S FATHER MATTHEW A 60 YEAR OLD WAS A CARING AND
LOVING MAN WHO HAD SHORT GREY HAIR AND BLACK EYES, WEARING
GREY TROUSERS AND A BLACK ROUND NECK JUMPER WAS IN THE
DINNER ROOM, WITH HIS 58 YEAR OLD WIFE SUSAN A BROWN
EYED WITH SHOULDER LENGTH GREY HAIR WEARING GLASSES, SHE
WAS WEARING BROWN TROUSERS WITH A V-NECK RED JUMPER WITH
FLAT BLACK SHOES.

MATTHEW AND SUSAN HAD BOTH PREPARED A BIRTHDAY PARTY FOR
THERE DAUGHTER IN THE DINNER ROOM THERE WAS A MEDIUM SIZE
BIRTHDAY CAKE, WITH ICING ON SAYING HAPPY 40TH BIRTHDAY
CATHY AND THERE WAS ONE CANDLE STUCK IN THE MIDDLE OF THE
CAKE.

SUSAN LOOKS AT MATTHEW AS HE WALKS INTO THE KITCHEN TO
PICK UP A SMALL BOX OF MATCHES, WHICH WAS NEXT TO THE
COOKER.

SUSAN SAYS TO MATTHEW "DO YOU THINK CATHY WILL LIKE THE
CAKE?"

MATTHEW WALKS OUT OF THE KITCHEN AND HE GOES TO THE DINNER
TABLE WHERE SUSAN WAS STANDING NEAR THE BIRTHDAY CAKE AND
SHE SAYS TO HIM "CATHY WILL LIKE THE BIRTHDAY CAKE."

SUSAN AND MATTHEW WERE BOTH LOOKING FORWARD TO SEEING
THEIR DAUGHTER, COMING HOME AND TO CELEBRATE HER BIRTHDAY
WITH HER.

CATHY WAS WALKING TOWARDS THE FRONT DOOR HOLDING THE BLUE
PLASTIC BOX IN HER RIGHT ARM AND SHE PRESSES THE DOORBELL,
WITH HER FINGER SHE STANDS THERE FOR 2 MINUTES AND SUSAN
OPENS THE DOOR WITH A SMILE, SHOWING HOW PROUD AND HAPPY
SHE WAS TO SEE HER DAUGHTER COME HOME.

CATHY LOOKS AT HER MOTHER'S HAPPINESS FOR HER AND SHE SAYS
TO HER "HI MUM."

MATTHEW WAS STANDING NEAR THE DINNER TABLE AND HE WAS HOLDING THE SMALL BOX OF MATCHES AND HE LIGHTS THE CANDLE THAT WAS ON THE CAKE, CATHY WAS IN THE LOUNGE AND SHE PUTS THE PLASTIC BOX, ON THE COFFEE TABLE AND SHE WALKS UP TO HER FATHER.

MATTHEW SAYS TO CATHY "HAPPY BIRTHDAY."

CATHY COULD SEE THAT HER PARENTS TOOK THE TIME AND EFFORT TO BUY HER A BIRTHDAY CAKE AND SHE SAYS "THANKS DAD."

SUSAN WALKS UP TO CATHY AND SHE HOLDS HER HAND, SHE SINGS HAPPY BIRTHDAY TO HER AND MATTHEW SINGS ALONG.

CATHY STANDS THERE STARING AT HER BIRTHDAY CAKE, SHE COULDN'T BELIEVE THAT SHE HAD TURNED 40 AND SO SHE BLOWS THE CANDLE.

SUSAN AND MATTHEW BOTH CLAP AND CHEER FOR CATHY WHILE SHE CUTS THE CAKE, WITH A SMALL SLIVER SHARP KNIFE AND SHE TAKES A SMALL PIECE TO EAT.

SUSAN GOES INTO THE KITCHEN AND SHE GOES TO THE TOP CUPBOARD TO GET 3 SMALL SIDE PLATES, SHE LEAVES THE KITCHEN AND WALKS TO THE DINNER TABLE, WHERE CATHY AND MATTHEW WERE BOTH SAT THERE.

CATHY SAYS TO HER PARENTS "YOU BOTH SHOULDN'T HAVE DONE THIS."

MATTHEW SAYS TO CATHY "DON'T BE SILLY. IT'S YOUR BIRTHDAY AND WE HAVE GOT YOU A FEW PRESENTS."

SUSAN PUTS THE 3 SMALL SIDE PLATES ON THE TABLE AND SHE SITS NEXT TO CATHY.

SUSAN SAYS TO CATHY "LET'S EAT A SLICE OF CAKE AND THEN WE WILL ORDER A PIZZA."

CATHY LOOKS UNHAPPY AND SAD AS SHE WANTED TO CELEBRATE HER BIRTHDAY IN STYLE.

LATER THAT EVENING MATTHEW AND SUSAN WERE BOTH IN THE KITCHEN STANDING THERE WAITING FOR THE KETTLE TO BOIL, SO

THEY CAN MAKE A CUP OF TEA AS THEY STAND THERE, THEY BOTH LOOKED WORRIED AND CONCERNED FOR THERE DAUGHTER.

SUSAN SAYS TO MATTHEW "I DON'T UNDERSTAND WHY CATHY IS SO UNHAPPY?"

SUSAN LOOKS AT HER HUSBAND AND SHE SAYS TO HIM "CATHY DOESN'T EVEN TELL US HER PROBLEMS."

MATTHEW COULD SEE SUSAN'S WORRIEDNESS FOR CATHY AND HE SAYS TO HER CALMLY "DON'T WORRY I'LL TALK TO HER."

SUSAN SAYS TO MATTHEW "CATHY HAS BEEN SINGLE FOR YEARS, SHE DOESN'T EVEN MAKE ANY FRIENDS."

SUSAN LOOKS STRESSED AND SHE HAD HER HEAD HELD DOWN, MATTHEW GIVES HER A HUG AND SHE HOLDS HIM.

MATTHEW SAYS TO SUSAN "CATHY WILL MAKE FRIENDS. YOU'LL SEE."

CATHY WAS UPSTAIRS IN HER BEDROOM WEARING HER BLACK NIGHTCLOTHES, SHE WAS LYING ON THE BED FEELING SAD AND LONELY AND SHE SITS UP FROM THE BED, SHE LOOKS AT HER WATCH FROM HER RIGHT WRIST AND IT WAS 10'OCLOCK AND SHE SAYS "I DON'T THINK I WILL EVER BE HAPPY."

CATHY TAKES A DEEP SIGH AND SHE LIES BACK IN THE BED, THINKING HOW SAD AND GREY HER LIFE WAS RIGHT NOW, HAVING NO ONE TO LAUGH AND JOKE WITH.


IT SOON CAME MORNING AND CATHY WAS STILL IN HER NIGHTCLOTHES AND SHE WALKS DOWN THE STAIRS, HER FATHER WAS IN THE LOUNGE SAT ON THE SOFA READING THE NEWSPAPER, SHE LOOKS AT HIM AND SHE SAYS TO HIM "MORNING DAD."

MATTHEW SAYS "MORNING CATHY."

CATHY WALKS INTO THE KITCHEN WHERE SUSAN WAS HOLDING A HOT CUP OF TEA.

CATHY SAYS TO SUSAN "MORNING MUM."

SUSAN SAYS "MORNING. ARE YOU GOING TO WORK TODAY?"

CATHY SAYS "NO IT'S MY DAY OFF."

CATHY GOES TO OPEN THE TOP CUPBOARD AND SHE TAKES A CUP OUT, SHE SHUTS THE CUPBOARD DOOR AND SHE PUTS THE KETTLE ON, SUSAN TAKES A SIP OF HER HOT TEA AND SHE PUTS THE CUP ON THE KITCHEN TABLE.

SUSAN SAYS TO CATHY "WE SHOULD GO SHOPPING."

CATHY WAS STANDING THERE WAITING FOR THE KETTLE TO BOIL; SHE DIDN'T REALLY WANT TO GO SHOPPING WITH HER MOTHER.

CATHY SAYS TO SUSAN "I DON'T WANT TO GO SHOPPING."

SUSAN SAYS "WHY?"

CATHY SAYS "I'LL JUST GET BORED."

SUSAN SAYS "NO YOU WON'T. I WANT TO SPEND TIME WITH YOU."

SUSAN SMILES AT CATHY AND SHE PICKS HER CUP OF WARM TEA UP FROM THE KITCHEN TABLE AND SHE WALKS OUT OF THE KITCHEN AND INTO THE LOUNGE.

CATHY WAS IN THE KITCHEN STANDING THERE HOLDING ONTO HER EMPTY CUP, HUFFING AND PUFFING ABOUT GOING SHOPPING WITH HER MOTHER, SHE HAD TO FORCE HERSELF TO GO BUT SHE DIDN'T WANT TO TELL HER PROBLEMS TO HER MOTHER.

IT WAS THE AFTERNOON SUSAN AND CATHY WERE BOTH IN TOWN WALKING IN THE STREET.

CATHY LOOKED MISERABLE WALKING WITH SUSAN IN THE STREET AND SHE SAYS TO HER "MUM CAN WE GO HOME NOW."

SUSAN SAYS "WE'VE ONLY BEEN HERE FOR HALF AN HOUR."

CATHY SAYS "BUT IT SEEMS LIKE WE HAVE BEEN HERE FOR HOURS."

SUSAN LINKS HER ARM WITH CATHY'S AND SHE COULD SEE THAT HER DAUGHTER WAS BEHAVING LIKE A 5 YEAR OLD.

SUSAN SAYS TO CATHY "YOU NEED TO CHILL OUT AND HAVE FUN."

AS CATHY WAS WALKING WITH SUSAN DOWN THE STREET GOING

PASS THE CLOTHES SHOPS, SHE DIDN'T WANT TO LISTEN TO WHAT HER MOTHER HAD TO SAY AND SHE IGNORES IT.

CATHY LIKED LIVING WITH SADNESS AND HAVING UNHAPPINESS IN HER LIFE, SHE DIDN'T WANT HER PARENTS TO CONTROL OR HAVE ANY PART OF GIVING HER JOY, HAPPINESS AND LOVE.

## Chapter Two
## <u>A New College Girl</u>

It was a Tuesday morning Tina a 22-year-old woman black eyed with brown long hair, wearing jeans a black v-neck t-shirt with black high heel shoes on, was holding her brown handbag and a exercise book in her left hand.

Tina was walking towards the college and it was 9.50 am, she was running late for her lesson being her first day.

Tina walks into the college as she walks inside she was feeling a bit nervous, she sees Cathy standing outside her classroom talking to a 20 year old geek male student.

Cathy says to the student "Make sure you finish of your course work. See you tomorrow."

The male student walks off and Tina walks up to Cathy.

Tina says to Cathy "Hi."

Cathy looks at Tina having no idea who she was and she says to her "And who are you?"

Tina says "I'm Tina."

Cathy says "My new student. Your late."

Tina says "I'm really sorry."

Cathy says "Not good for your first day."

Tina looked worried and she was hoping that Cathy wouldn't tell her off.

Cathy says to Tina "Go and sit down."

Tina smiles at Cathy and she walks in the classroom.

During the lesson Tina was sat at her desk there were 14 students there reading the book of Romeo & Juliet.

Cathy was standing near her desk holding the book of Romeo

& JULIET IN ONE HAND AND A NEW EXERCISE BOOK IN THE OTHER; SHE GOES UP TO TINA TO GIVE HER BOOK.

CATHY LOOKS AT HER STUDENTS AND SHE SAYS TO THEM "NOW I KNOW YOU HAVE ALL STARTED READING THE BOOK. AND I AM GOING TO GIVE YOU THE COURSE WORK TO DO."

CATHY TURNS AROUND AND SHE WALKS UP TO HER DESK WHERE SHE PICKS UP 15 PAPERS, OF QUESTIONS ABOUT THE BOOK OF ROMEO & JULIET, SHE GOES UP TO EACH STUDENT IN THE CLASS GIVING THEM A PAPER EACH SUDDENLY THE BELL RINGS AT 10 O'CLOCK. THE STUDENTS GET UP FROM THEIR CHAIRS AND THEY PUT THEIR EXERCISE BOOK AND PAPER IN THEIR BAG AND THEY LEAVE THE CLASSROOM.

TINA WAS HOLDING A ROMEO & JULIET BOOK AND A QUESTION PAPER IN HER HAND AND CATHY WALKS UP TO HER DESK.

TINA LOOKS AT CATHY AND SHE SAYS TO HER "BYE MADAM."

CATHY LOOKS AT TINA AND SHE SAYS "BYE."

TINA WALKS OUT OF THE CLASSROOM AND CATHY LOOKS AT HER, BUT SHE WASN'T SURE ABOUT HER BEING IN HER CLASS, WANTING TO LEARN AS SHE HAD CAME LATE FOR HER FIRST LESSON.

LATER THAT EVENING AS THE SUN WAS GOING DOWN IN SAN FRANCISCO, CATHY WAS AT HOME IN THE LOUNGE SAT ON THE SOFA NEXT TO HER MUM, THEY WERE BOTH WATCHING BAREFOOT CONTESSA ON T.V.

SUSAN SAYS TO CATHY "HOW WAS YOUR DAY?"

CATHY SAYS "IT WAS OK I HAVE A NEW STUDENT IN MY CLASS. HER NAME IS TINA. SHE'S A NICE PERSON."

SUSAN WAS PLEASED THAT HER DAUGHTER HAD MADE A NEW FRIEND AND SHE SAYS TO CATHY "WHY DON'T YOU ASK HER TO COME ROUND."

CATHY WAS SHOCKED OF WHAT HER MUM HAD SAID TO HER AND SHE LOOKS AT HER AND SHE SAYS "I DON'T THINK SO."

Susan says to Cathy "You need to make friends."

Cathy says "Yes I know I need a friend but not one of my students. I'm going to bed. Goodnight."

Cathy gets up from the sofa and she didn't like her mum's opinion, about how she could make things better for her.

Cathy gets up from the sofa and she leaves the lounge and she walks up the stairs, she goes into her bedroom waiting for the morning to arrive, so she can go to work and be left alone.

The next day Cathy was outside the college and students were sat on the grass, talking and eating there lunch several students were walking and talking to each other.

Tina sees Cathy sat on the bench watching the students and she walks up to her.

Tina says to Cathy "Hi Madam."

Cathy says "Hello."

Tina says to Cathy "You're a quite person. You don't smile or look happy. Why?"

Cathy says "Because I like being miserable. Now can you leave me alone."

Tina says "No."

Tina goes to sit next to Cathy to try and find out what's wrong with her.

Cathy knew that Tina was trying to be her friend and so she gives her the cold shoulder.

Cathy says to Tina "Why have you sat next to me."

Tina says "Because I like you."

Cathy didn't want Tina to know about her life and she tries to shut her away.

Cathy says to Tina "I don't want you to like me. I just want to be left alone."

TINA SAYS "WHY? TALK TO ME."

CATHY SAYS "YOU'RE MY STUDENT AND I DON'T WANT TO TALK TO YOU ABOUT MY LIFE."

CATHY GETS UP FROM THE BENCH AND SHE WALKS INTO THE COLLEGE, TINA SITS THERE AND SHE KNEW THAT SHE HAD TO DO SOMETHING TO HELP HER TEACHER, TO LIVE LIFE AND SHE TAKES A SIGH.

THE NEXT THING CATHY WAS IN HER CLASSROOM AND SHE WAS HOLDING, 3 TEXTBOOKS IN HER HAND AND SHE PUTS THEM ON THE MIDDLE SHELF, TINA WALKS IN AND SHE SAYS TO HER "HI MADAM."

CATHY TURNS AROUND TO LOOK AT TINA AND SHE DIDN'T LOOK PLEASED TO SEE HER.

CATHY SAYS TO TINA "NOT YOU AGAIN. I THOUGHT YOU HAD GONE HOME."

TINA SAYS "I KNOW YOU WANT TO TALK TO SOMEONE."

CATHY SAYS "IF I WANTED TO SHARE MY PROBLEMS WITH SOMEONE I WOULD. BUT IT ISN'T GOING TO BE YOU."

TINA COULD SEE CATHY'S ANGER AND FRUSTRATION AND SHE WALKS UP TO HER TO CALM HER DOWN, SHE LOOKS INTO HER EYES AND SHE SAYS TO HER "YOU'RE A SAD AND LONELY WOMAN."

CATHY SAYS TO TINA "EXCUSE ME."

TINA SAYS "I'M RIGHT THOUGH."

CATHY SAYS "IT DOESN'T CONCERN YOU. WHY DO YOU CARE?"

TINA SAYS "BECAUSE I WANT TO BE YOUR FRIEND."

CATHY SAYS "SORRY BUT I DON'T MAKE FRIENDS."

CATHY WALKS UP TO HER DESK TO PICK UP HER BLACK ROSITTI HANDBAG AND SHE LEAVES THE CLASSROOM.

TINA WAS LEFT IN THE CLASSROOM STANDING THERE THINKING OF A WAY TO BE PART OF CATHY'S LIFE.

LATER IN THE DAY CATHY WAS WITH HER MUM AND THEY WERE

BOTH IN TOWN IN THE COFFEE SHOP, THEY WERE BOTH SAT ON THE SOFA HOLDING A CUP EACH OF WARM COFFEE.

CATHY WAS SAT THERE HOLDING HER CUP OF COFFEE LOOKING ANGRY AT TINA'S KINDNESS, WHICH HAD MADE FEEL AWKWARD SUSAN COULD SEE HER DAUGHTER'S MOODY FACE.

SUSAN SAYS TO CATHY "WHAT'S WRONG? WHY ARE YOU ANGRY?"

CATHY SAYS "I'M NOT ANGRY."

SUSAN SAYS "IT'S THAT GIRL FROM COLLEGE."

CATHY LOOKS AT HER MUM AND SHE TELLS HER THE PROBLEMS SHE HAS.

CATHY SAYS TO SUSAN "TINA IS SO IRRITATING. I HATE HER."

SUSAN SAYS "WHAT DID SHE SAY TO YOU."

CATHY SAYS "SHE WANTS TO KNOW ME SHE SAID I AM SAD AND LONELY. AND TINA WANTS TO BE MY FRIEND."

SUSAN SAYS "SHE'S ONLY BEING NICE TO YOU."

CATHY SAYS "WELL I'M NOT HAVING IT."

CATHY TAKES A SIP OF HER CUP OF WARM COFFEE AND SUSAN WANTED HER DAUGHTER, TO BE FRIENDS WITH TINA AND TO BE HAPPY AGAIN.

WILL CATHY LET TINA BE IN HER LIFE?

LATER THAT NIGHT CATHY WAS AT HOME UPSTAIRS IN HER BEDROOM AND SHE WAS WEARING, HER WHITE NIGHTCLOTHES AND SHE WAS IN THE BED BESIDE HER, WAS A SMALL ROUND TABLE WITH A BLUE MEDIUM SIZE DIARY NEXT TO A BLUE PEN, A LAMP NEXT TO IT WAS A SMALL ALARM CLOCK WHICH WAS TICKING AT 10 O'CLOCK.

MATTHEW KNOCKS ON THE DOOR AND CATHY SAYS "COME IN."

MATTHEW OPENS THE DOOR TO SEE CATHY IN THE BED AND HE SAYS TO HER "ARE YOU ALRIGHT."

CATHY LOOKS AT HER DAD AND SHE SAYS TO HIM "I'M FINE."

MATTHEW WALKS INTO THE BEDROOM AND HE GOES TO SIT ON THE BED, CATHY SITS UP FROM THE BED AND THEY BOTH LOOK AT EACH OTHER, THIS WAS A TIME FOR A FATHER AND DAUGHTER TALK.

MATTHEW SAYS TO CATHY "I'M WORRIED ABOUT YOU."

CATHY SAYS "WHY ARE YOU WORRIED ABOUT ME DAD?"

MATTHEW SAYS "BECAUSE I THINK YOUR GOING TO BE LEFT ON YOUR OWN FOREVER."

CATHY SAYS "DAD I'M NOT ON MY OWN. I HAVE YOU AND MUM."

MATTHEW SAYS "I MEAN A PARTNER OR A FRIEND. EVERYONE NEEDS SOMEONE IN THERE LIFE."

CATHY SAYS "I KNOW YOU WANT ME TO BE HAPPY AGAIN. BUT I DON'T THINK THAT WILL HAPPEN AGAIN."

CATHY LEANS BACK IN THE BED AND MATTHEW GETS UP AND HE SAYS TO HER "GOODNIGHT."

MATTHEW LEAVES CATHY'S ROOM AND HE SHUTS THE DOOR, HE TAKES A DEEP SIGH OF WORRY AND FEAR FOR HIS DAUGHTER'S FUTURE.

CATHY WAS LYING IN THE BED AND SHE FELT UNHAPPY ABOUT HER LIFE, HER DAD WAS RIGHT ABOUT HER AND SHE HAD TEARS IN HER EYES OF THE LONELINESS SHE HAD, SHE WAS YEARNING FOR

FRIENDSHIP, HAPPINESS AND LOVE.

WILL CATHY TAKE A CHANCE TO MAKE FRIENDS WITH TINA?

## Chapter Three
## Let's Be Friends

Tina was in college in her English lesson and she was sat at her desk, with 14 other students writing an essay about Shakespeare, Cathy was standing near the black board watching them like a hawk.

Tina looks at Cathy and she gives her a wave.

Cathy says "Tina."

Tina carries on writing her essay the bell rings and the students stop writing, they pack their books into their bags and they get up to leave the classroom.

Tina holds her book and paper in her hand and she gets up from the chair, she sees Cathy standing near the desk looking at a few papers, which were written by the students about Romeo & Juliet.

Tina walks up to Cathy and she says to her "Madam."

Cathy looks at Tina and she was not keen of what she was going to say to her.

Tina says to Cathy "I was thinking if you would like to have lunch with me?"

Cathy was shocked and she didn't want to hang out with Tina.

Cathy says to Tina "Go to lunch. With you."

Tina says "Yeah. Why not."

Tina could see Cathy thinking about weather to go to lunch with her, she was hoping for a positive reply.

Cathy says to Tina "Ok I will go to lunch with you."

Tina smiles at Cathy and she was pleased that she had a

CHANGE OF HEART.

TINA SAYS TO CATHY "GREAT."

TINA AND CATHY BOTH LEAVE THE CLASSROOM TOGETHER AS THIS WAS A NEW BEGINNING OF FRIENDSHIP.


THE NEXT THING TINA AND CATHY WERE BOTH IN TOWN AND THEY WERE SAT OUTSIDE THE COFFEE SHOP WAITING FOR THERE MEAL TO ARRIVE, THEY HAD A CUP EACH OF HOT CHOCOLATE AND A FEW CHOCOLATE CHIP COOKIES ON A SMALL FLAT PLATE.

CATHY SAYS TO TINA "WHY DO YOU WANT TO TALK TO ME?"

TINA SAYS "BECAUSE YOU LOOK UNHAPPY WHENEVER I SEE YOU. YOU DON'T EVEN TALK TO THE TEACHERS."

CATHY SAYS "I DON'T HAVE ANY FRIENDS. I'M JUST A LONER."

TINA SAYS "YOUR NOT A LONER. YOU DO HAVE A FRIEND."

CATHY LOOKS AT TINA KNOWING THAT SHE COULD TALK TO HER AND THAT WAS HAPPINESS FOR HER.

BUT HOW LONG WILL IT LAST?

WILL IT BE HAPPINESS FOR CATHY OR A JOURNEY OF TEARS AND GRIEF?


4 MONTHS LATER IT WAS CHRISTMAS AND CATHY WAS IN TOWN, SHE WAS WALKING IN THE BUSY STREET, SHE COULD SEE PEOPLE BUYING PRESENTS FOR FRIENDS AND FAMILY, AS IT WAS THE MOST JOYFUL TIME OF THE YEAR.

FOR CATHY IT HAD BEEN FOUR MONTHS AND SHE FELT HAPPIER. SHE SMILED AND LAUGHED AND SHE WAS GLAD, TO HAVE MADE FRIENDS WITH TINA.

CATHY WAS WALKING PASS THE CHINESE RESTAURANT WHEN SHE SEES TINA, STANDING OUTSIDE THE STAR BUCKS COFFEE SHOP WAITING FOR HER.

CATHY SHOUTS "HI TINA."

CATHY WALKS UP TO TINA AND THEY BOTH GIVE EACH OTHER A HUG, THEY BOTH WALK INSIDE THE COFFEE SHOP TO CHAT ABOUT THEIR DAY.

LATER THAT EVENING TINA WAS ROUND CATHY'S HOUSE AND SHE WAS IN THE LOUNGE SAT ON THE SOFA, SUSAN AND MATTHEW WERE BOTH SAT ON THE OTHER SOFA AND THEY WERE BOTH LOOKING HAPPY.

SUSAN SAYS TO TINA "IT'S THE FIRST TIME THAT CATHY HAS BROUGHT A FRIEND ROUND."

MATTHEW SAY TO TINA "ARE YOU HUNGRY?"

TINA LOOKS AT SUSAN AND MATTHEW AND SHE SAYS TO THEM "NO I'M FINE THANKS."

CATHY WALKS INTO THE LOUNGE AND SHE LOOKS AT TINA AND SHE SAYS TO HER "SHALL WE GO."

SUSAN SAYS TO CATHY "AREN'T YOU GOING TO SHOW TINA YOUR ROOM."

CATHY LOOKS AT HER PARENTS AND SHE WAS EMBARRASSED OF THEM AND SHE SAYS "MUM I'M NOT FIVE. I DON'T THINK TINA WOULD WANT TO SEE MY ROOM."

TINA SAYS TO CATHY "I WOULD LOVE TO SEE YOUR BEDROOM."

THE NEXT THING TINA WAS UPSTAIRS WITH CATHY IN THE BEDROOM.

CATHY SAYS TO TINA "NOW YOU'VE SEEN MY ROOM SHALL WE GO DOWNSTAIRS."

TINA LOOKS AROUND CATHY'S ROOM AND SHE SPOTS A BLUE DIARY ON THE TABLE NEXT TO THE BED.

TINA WAS CURIOUS TO KNOW CATHY'S HIDDEN SECRETS AND SHE WAS WAITING TO TAKE THE DIARY TO READ.

CATHY SAYS TO TINA "I'M JUST GOING TO THE BATHROOM."

CATHY LEAVES THE ROOM AND SHE WALKS TO THE BATHROOM AND SHE SHUTS THE DOOR, TINA WAS IN HER ROOM AND SHE GOES UP TO THE TABLE AND SHE PICKS UP THE BLUE DIARY TO READ, BUT

THEN SHE HAD AN IDEA AND SHE OPENS HER HANDBAG AND SNEAKS IT INTO HER BAG, SHE LEAVES THE ROOM AND SHE SHUTS THE DOOR.

CATHY OPENS THE BATHROOM DOOR AND SHE WALKS OUT AND TINA LOOKS AT HER.

TINA SAYS TO CATHY "SHALL WE GO DOWNSTAIRS."

THE NEXT THING CATHY AND TINA WERE BOTH IN TOWN WALKING IN THE STREET, THERE WAS A FEW CHINESE AND ITALIAN RESTAURANTS OPEN ACROSS THE STREET.

CATHY SAYS TO TINA "SHALL GO TO A RESTAURANT."

BUT TINA HAD OTHER PLANS AND THAT WAS TO GO HOME AND READ CATHY'S DIARY.

TINA SAYS TO CATHY "NO I DON'T WANT TO EAT. LET'S JUST GO FOR A WALK AROUND TOWN."

CATHY WAS HAPPY TO WALK AND TALK WITH TINA.

LATER THAT NIGHT TINA WAS AT HER ONE BEDROOM APARTMENT AND SHE WAS IN HER BEDROOM SAT ON THE BED, HOLDING CATHY'S BLUE DIARY IN HER HAND, SHE WAS THINKING WEATHER TO READ IT OR NOT, SO SHE OPENS THE DIARY AND STARTS READING HER FRIEND'S SECRETS.

WHILE TINA WAS READING CATHY'S DIARY SHE FELT SAD AND SHE HAD TEARS IN HER EYES AND SO SHE SHUTS, THE DIARY AND PUTS IT CLOSE TO HER CHEST, IT WAS LIKE SHE WANTED TO FEEL THE PAIN FROM HER FRIEND.

TINA CRIES, AS SHE KNEW THAT SHE HAD TO DO SOMETHING ABOUT CATHY'S LIFE BEFORE IT'S TOO LATE.

WHAT IS CATHY HIDING?

WILL TINA'S PLAN SUCCEED?

IS SOMEONE GOING TO WALK INTO CATHY AND TINA'S LIFE?

**16**

Chapter Four
A Friend From The Past

Cathy was at home and it was **11** o'clock in the morning and she was upstairs in her bedroom, looking and searching for her blue diary, she was frustrated and fed up and she says to herself "I can't believe I've lost my diary. Where can it be?"

Downstairs Susan was in the lounge standing there waiting, for her daughter to come down and she shouts "Cathy are you ready!"

Cathy walks down the stairs looking angry and worried about her missing diary and she goes into the lounge.

Susan looks at Cathy and she could see, her daughter was stressed about something.

Susan says to Cathy "What's wrong?"

Cathy says to Susan "Mum I can't find my diary."

Susan says "It's probably in one of your draws in your room or check under the bed."

Cathy looks at her mum and she thinks that she has taken her diary, to read and so she asks her help to find where it is.

Cathy says to Susan "Have you taken my diary?"

Susan was shocked that Cathy thought it was her, she would never go through her daughter's personal stuff.

Susan says to Cathy "I haven't taken your diary."

Suddenly Cathy had some idea of who had taken her diary and she says "It must be Tina."

22

CATHY STORMS OUT OF THE LOUNGE AND SHE RUNS UPSTAIRS TO HER BEDROOM, WHERE HER MOBILE WAS ON THE BED AND SHE PICKS IT UP, TO CALL TINA BUT IT WENT ON VOICE MAIL.

LATER IN THE DAY CATHY WAS AT HOME IN THE LOUNGE SAT ON THE SOFA READING A WOMAN'S MAGAZINE, WHEN THE DOOR BELL RINGS AND SHE PUTS THE MAGAZINE ON THE COFFEE TABLE, SHE GETS UP FROM THE SOFA AND SHE GOES TO ANSWER THE FRONT DOOR, TINA WAS STANDING THERE AND SHE SAYS TO HER "HI CATHY."

CATHY LOOKS AT TINA AND SHE WAS PLEASED TO SEE HER BUT SHE DIDN'T LOOK HAPPY, BECAUSE SHE KNEW THAT SHE HAD TAKEN HER DIARY.

CATHY SAYS "COME IN TINA."

TINA WALKS IN AND CATHY SHUTS THE FRONT DOOR AND SHE WAS READY TO CONFRONT HER ABOUT HER DIARY.

WHEN TINA OPENS HER HANDBAG AND SHE TAKES THE DIARY OUT TO GIVE TO CATHY.

TINA SAYS TO CATHY "HERE'S YOUR DIARY."

CATHY WAS SHOCKED AND SHE TAKES THE DIARY OFF TINA'S HAND AND SHE SAYS TO HER "WHY DID YOU TAKE MY DIARY. IT WAS PRIVATE."

TINA SAYS "I'M SORRY I TOOK YOUR DIARY BUT I WAS CONCERNED ABOUT YOU. NOW I KNOW WHY YOU ARE UNHAPPY IN YOUR LIFE."

CATHY STANDS THERE KNOWING THAT SOMEBODY CLOSE TO HER FINALLY KNEW HOW SHE FELT EMOTIONALLY IN HER LIFE.

TINA SAYS TO CATHY "YOU LOST YOUR HUSBAND."

CATHY FELT HEART BROKEN TO HEAR WHAT TINA HAD SAID AND SHE SAYS TO HER "HE HAD CANCER. AND THERE WAS NOTHING I COULD DO FOR HIM. I LOVED HIM BUT EVEN THAT WASN'T ENOUGH AND NOW I'M ALL ALONE."

TINA LOOKS AT CATHY'S FACE AND SHE COULD SEE THE GRIEF AND SORROW SHE HAD.

TINA SAYS TO CATHY "YOUR NOT ON YOUR OWN. I'M HERE FOR YOU."

TINA GIVES CATHY A WARM HUG.


LATER THAT EVENING DAVID A 38-YEAR-OLD MAN TALL WITH SHORT BROWN HAIR AND BROWN EYES, A SLIM BUILD WEARING JEANS AND BLACK SHIRT AND BLACK SHOES, WAS IN THE LOUNGE WITH MATTHEW AND THEY WERE BOTH STANDING NEAR THE DINNER TABLE, BOTH HOLDING A GLASS EACH OF RED WINE.

MATTHEW SAYS TO DAVID " ARE YOU STILL WORKING FOR BMW?"

DAVID SAYS "YES. I'VE WORKED THERE FOR 6 YEARS. THEY'RE PAYING ME GOOD MONEY. AND THEY GAVE ME A DISCOUNT FOR THE CAR I BROUGHT."

MATTHEW SAYS "THAT'S GOOD. DO YOU HAVE A GIRLFRIEND?"

DAVID SAYS "NO I'M SINGLE. AND I'M TOO BUSY WITH WORK."

MATTHEW SAYS "YOUR JUST LIKE MY DAUGHTER."

CATHY, TINA AND SUSAN WERE IN THE KITCHEN WAITING FOR THE LARGE WHOLE CHICKEN TO COOK, IN THE OVEN ALONG WITH A LARGE TRAY OF ROAST POTATOES, CHOPPED CARROTS AND CAULIFLOWER IN A LARGE PAN TO BOIL ON THE COOKER IN A LOW HEAT. THEY WERE STANDING NEAR THE TABLE DRINKING A GLASS EACH OF WHITE WINE.

SUSAN SAYS TO CATHY "I'M GLAD DAVID HAS COME TO SEE YOU. YOU NEED A MALE FRIEND TO TALK TO."

CATHY SAYS TO SUSAN "SHOULDN'T WE CHECK THE FOOD."

TINA TAKES A SIP OF HER GLASS OF WHITE WINE, SUSAN GOES TO OPEN THE OVEN TO SEE THE CHICKEN AND POTATOES AND IT WAS HALF COOKED, SHE SHUTS THE OVEN DOOR.

Susan says to Cathy "It's nearly cooked."

Cathy says "Great."

Cathy wanted to get away from her mum and she looks at Tina "Shall we go in the living room."

Tina says "Ok."

Tina and Cathy both leave the kitchen and they walk into the lounge, where David and Matthew were sat at the dinner table chatting about, buying and selling cars in the auction and they both look at them.

Cathy says to David "This is my friend Tina."

Tina says to David "Hi."

David says "Hello."

Cathy says to David "Tina is in my class."

David says to Tina "So how long are you studying for?"

Tina says to David "A year."

David says to Tina "That's good."

Susan shouts in the kitchen so Cathy, Tina, David and Matthew could hear.

Susan says "Cathy could you come in the kitchen and help me!"

Cathy puts her glass of white wine on the table and she goes to the kitchen, Tina goes to sit opposite David and he looks, at her and smiles he had a liking for her.

Cathy was in the kitchen helping her mum prepare the food on a large dish, which had roast chicken, roast potatoes and vegetables.

The next thing Cathy, Susan, David, Tina and Matthew were sat at the dinner table eating their plate of roast potatoes, a piece of roast chicken with vegetables and gravy and they were all enjoying their meal.

Later that evening Cathy was outside her house and she was

WAVING AT TINA WHO WAS IN A TAXI, THE 30-YEAR-OLD ASIAN TAXI MAN DRIVES OFF, SHE GOES INSIDE THE HOUSE AND SHE SHUTS THE FRONT DOOR.

CATHY WALKS IN THE LOUNGE WHERE DAVID WAS SAT ON THE SOFA WAITING FOR HER TO COME CHAT TO HIM, SHE GOES TO SIT NEXT TO HIM.

DAVID SAYS TO CATHY "YOUR FRIEND SEEMS NICE."

CATHY SAYS "SHE'S A NICE GIRL. SO TELL ME. WHY HAVE COME HERE?"

DAVID LOOKS AT CATHY AND HE COULDN'T UNDERSTAND WHY SHE WASN'T PLEASED TO SEE HIM.

DAVID SAYS TO CATHY "BECAUSE YOU'RE MY FRIEND AND I LIKE YOU. I'VE MISSED YOU."

CATHY SAYS "SORRY I THOUGHT YOU'VE STOPPED CARING ABOUT ME."

DAVID GIVES CATHY A WARM A HUG AND SHE SMILES FOR HAVING HIM THERE BY HER SIDE.

THE NEXT DAY DAVID WAS OUTSIDE THE COLLEGE WAITING FOR CATHY, TINA WALKS OUT OF THE COLLEGE WITH A FEW MALE STUDENTS FROM HER CLASS, SHE SEES HIM STANDING THERE WAITING AND THEY BOTH LOOK AT EACH OTHER AND SMILE.

DAVID GOES UP TO TINA AND HE SAYS TO HER "HI."

TINA SAYS "HI DAVID."

DAVID SAYS TO TINA "HOW WAS YOUR LESSON?"

TINA SAYS "IT WAS ALRIGHT. SO HOW LONG HAVE YOU KNOWN CATHY?"

DAVID SAYS "12 YEARS. I MET CATHY IN A MBA CLASS."

DAVID WANTED TO KNOW MORE ABOUT TINA AND HE SAYS TO HER "DO YOU WANT TO GO FOR LUNCH TOMORROW?"

TINA SAYS "OK."

DAVID SAYS "I'LL SEE YOU HERE TOMORROW."

Tina says "Cool see you then. Bye."

David says "Bye."

Tina walks off and David watches her when Cathy walks out of the college and she sees him.

Cathy says to David "Hey."

David turns around and he looks at Cathy and he smiles at her and he says "Hi."

Cathy looks at David and he gives her a hug and he looks at her and he says "How are you."

Cathy says "I'm fine. Shall we get a bite to eat."

David says "Ok."

David and Cathy both walk off together and they cross the road and walk in the street.

The next thing Cathy and David were at Sub way and they both sat at the small round table, both eating a ham and salad sandwich each with a can of Coke Cola.

Later that night Cathy was at home and she was in her bedroom wearing her white night clothes, lying on the bed reading a book called Pride & Prejudice, it was like she wanted to be loved. But she felt scared because eight years ago her husband died of cancer and she could never be with anyone.

As the night falls and the sun raises over San Francisco

it was afternoon Tina and David were both walking together in the park.

David says to Tina "So what do you do in your free time?"

Tina says "Well I like playing football with my friends and I like travelling."

David looks at Tina and he says to her "Really so do

I."

Tina looks at David and she smiles at him as the two were both walking together in the park, they both talk about what they liked and disliked about food, colour and films. They had a lot in common this was a new beginning of friendship for Tina and David.

Could there be love for Tina, Cathy and David?

## Chapter Five
## The Love Begins

It's autumn in San Francisco and the love walks into Cathy, Tina and David's life, but will it be true and lasting love for them?

It was a Sunday evening Tina was wearing a short black sexy dress with black high heel shoes on, David was wearing black trousers and a red shirt with black shoes on and they were both, walking together at the Golden Gate Bridge, it is one of the worlds most famous landmarks. David had something to say to Tina and he couldn't wait any longer to tell her.
David says to Tina "I have fallen in love with you."
Tina turns to look at David and she says to him "I feel the same way."
Tina and David both give each other a hug and they both gaze, into each other's eyes and they have a passionate kiss.

This was a new beginning of love for Tina and David but will it last?

The next morning Cathy was at home and she was in her bedroom wearing, a red v-neck top and a black skit with black high heel shoes on, she was ready to go out and to see David and she was feeling happy within herself, she looks at her alarm clock that was on the table next to her

29

BED IT WAS 1.30 PM, SHE LEAVES HER ROOM AND SHE GOES DOWNSTAIRS AND SHE GOES TO OPEN THE FRONT DOOR, SHE WALKS OUT OF THE HOUSE AND SHE SHUTS THE DOOR.

DAVID WAS IN TOWN HOLDING A BUNCH OF PINK ROSES AND HE WAS STANDING OUTSIDE THE COFFEE SHOP WAITING FOR CATHY. 20 MINUTES LATER CATHY WAS IN TOWN AND SHE WAS WALKING IN THE STREET WITH A SMILE AND SHE SEES DAVID, WAITING FOR HER HOLDING A BUNCH OF PINK ROSES, SHE GOES UP TO HIM TO FIND OUT WHY HE WAS IN A HAPPY MOOD.

CATHY SAYS TO DAVID "HIYA."

DAVID SAYS "HI."

DAVID GIVES CATHY A HUG AND HE GIVES HER THE BUNCH OF PINK ROSES TO HER, SHE TAKES THEM WITH LOVE AND SHE SMILES AT HIM.

DAVID SAYS TO CATHY "SHALL WE HAVE LUNCH."

CATHY SAYS "OK."

DAVID PUTS HIS ARM AROUND CATHY AND THEY BOTH WALK INTO THE COFFEE SHOP, TO HAVE A CUP OF COFFEE AND SHE THINKS THAT HE HAS FEELINGS FOR HER.

LATER THAT EVENING TINA WAS HOLDING A BUNCH OF RED ROSES IN HER HAND AND DAVID HAD HIS ARM AROUND HER, AS THEY WERE BOTH WALKING TOGETHER IN THE SANDY BEACH WATCHING THE SEA, MOVING BACKWARDS AND FORWARDS THERE RELATIONSHIP HAD JUST BEGUN AND THEY WERE HAPPY TOGETHER.

CATHY WAS AT HOME UPSTAIRS IN HER ROOM SAT ON THE BED THINKING, ABOUT DAVID AND HOW LOVING HE WAS TOWARDS HER THAT AFTERNOON, SHE PICKS UP THE BUNCH OF PINK ROSES NEXT TO HER, SHE LOOKS AT THEM AND SHE COULDN'T HELP, BUT TO SMILE WITH HAPPINESS IT WAS LIKE THE LOVE HAD TAKEN OVER HER LIFE ONCE AGAIN.

AS THE SUN WAS GOING DOWN IN LOVING AND HAPPY SAN

Francisco Cathy, Tina and David had there heart set on one person.

The next morning Cathy was in college in the classroom sat at her desk, marking her students homework of Romeo & Juliet.

Tina walks into the classroom and she looks at Cathy and she says "Hi Madam."

Cathy turns to look at Tina and she smiles at her and she says "Hiya."

Tina says to Cathy "Are you free later?"

Cathy says "No I'm going out with David."

Tina says "Ok. Well have fun."

Cathy says "We can meet up tomorrow evening."

Tina says "Cool see you then bye."

Cathy says "Bye Tina."

Tina turns around and she leaves the classroom and Cathy looks at her mobile that was near her paper, she picks it up to text David what time he was coming round to pick her up.

Tina walks out of the college and she sees David in his blue BMW 328i sat there waiting for her, she was pleased to see him and she walks up to the car.

Tina opens the car door and she gets in and she shuts the door, David gives her a kiss on the cheek and he says to her "Hey baby."

Tina says "Hi David."

David says "Shall I drop you off home."

Tina says "No let's go to your place."

David says "Ok. Later I'm seeing Cathy."

Tina says "That's cool."

David drives off and Cathy walks out of the college

HOLDING A FEW EXERCISE BOOKS IN HER HAND, SHE WAS FEELING EXCITED TO SEE HER FRIEND IN THE EVENING, SHE WALKS IN THE HURRY TO GO HOME SO SHE CAN, HAVE A SHOWER AND WEAR HER BEST CLOTHES TO GO OUT LATER.

LATER THAT EVENING CATHY WAS AT HOME STANDING AT THE TOP OF THE STAIRS, WEARING A SEXY BLACK DRESS WITH BLACK HIGH HEEL SHOES ON, SHE WALKS DOWN THE STAIRS AND SUSAN WAS IN THE LOUNGE SAT ON THE SOFA WATCHING T.V, SHE SEES HER DAUGHTER LOOKING BEAUTIFUL SUDDENLY THE DOOR BELL RINGS.

CATHY GOES TO OPEN THE FRONT DOOR AND IT WAS DAVID AND THEY BOTH SMILE AT EACH OTHER.

CATHY SAYS TO DAVID "HI."

DAVID SAYS "HI."

CATHY SAYS "COME IN."

DAVID SAYS "NO. LET'S GO OUT."

CATHY SAYS "OK."

DAVID TURNS AROUND AND HE WALKS TO HIS CAR, CATHY WAS IN THE HOUSE AND SHE LOOKS AT HER MUM.

CATHY SAYS TO SUSAN "MUM I'M GOING OUT. SEE YOU LATER."

SUSAN SAYS "BYE."

CATHY WALKS OUT OF THE HOUSE AND SHE SHUTS THE FRONT DOOR AND SHE GOES TO DAVID'S CAR.


LATER THAT NIGHT DAVID AND CATHY WERE BOTH WALKING TOGETHER IN THE SANDY BEACH.

CATHY SAYS TO DAVID "THANK YOU FOR TAKING ME TO DINNER."

DAVID SAYS "YOUR WELCOME. I'VE ENJOYED GOING OUT WITH YOU."

CATHY LOOKS AT DAVID AND SHE SMILES AT HIM AND SHE HAD A KIND OF A CRUSH ON HIM, THEY BOTH CARRY ON WALKING TOGETHER WATCHING THE SEA, THEY BOTH LOOK UP AT THE FULL

MOON HIGH UP AT THE NIGHT SKY, TINA WAS AT HER ONE BEDROOM APARTMENT STANDING OUTSIDE THE TERRACE TAKING SOME FRESH AIR, SHE WAS MISSING DAVID AND SHE WANTED TO BE IN HIS ARMS, SHE HAD HER MOBILE IN HER HAND AND SHE TEXT HIM SAYING I LOVE YOU.

DAVID WAS AT HOME IN HIS ROOM LYING ON THE BED LOOKING AT HIS MOBILE, READING THE TEXT THAT TINA HAD SENT AND HE SMILES AND HE SAYS "I LOVE YOU TOO."

THE NEXT MORNING TINA AND CATHY WERE BOTH OUTSIDE THE COLLEGE AND THE STUDENTS WERE WALKING OUT TO HAVE THEIR 15 MINUTE BREAK.

TINA AND CATHY WERE BOTH WALKING TOGETHER TOWARDS THE BENCH, BOTH LOOKING HAPPY AND EXCITED BEING IN LOVE WITH DAVID.

TINA SAYS TO CATHY "SO WHERE DID YOU AND DAVID GO."

CATHY SAYS "WE WENT TO A CHINESE RESTAURANT AND THEN WE WENT FOR A WALK IN THE BEACH. IT WAS ROMANTIC."

TINA LOOKS AT CATHY AND SHE THEN KNEW THAT SHE HAD FALLEN IN LOVE WITH DAVID.

CATHY SAYS TO TINA "I'VE FALLEN IN LOVE WITH DAVID."

CATHY LOOKS AT TINA AND SHE HOLDS HER WITH EXCITEMENT.

TINA WAS HOLDING CATHY IN HER ARMS, LOOKING SHOCKED AND DEVASTATED, AS SHE COULD NOT HELP BUT TO HAVE TEARS IN HER EYES.

WHO WILL HAVE A BROKEN HEART?

COULD IT BE TINA OR CATHY?

## Chapter Six
## FADING LOVE

IT'S THE 1<sup>ST</sup> OF SEPTEMBER AND CATHY WAS IN THE COLLEGE IN THE CLASSROOM ALONE AND SHE WAS STANDING NEAR THE WINDOW, SHE TURNS TO LOOK AT THE TREE THAT HAD DRY CRISPY LEAFS FALLING, SHE WAS MISSING TINA AS SHE HAD NOT BEEN ATTENDING HER LESSONS FOR THE PAST WEEK.

CATHY WAS WORRIED AND CONCERNED ABOUT TINA AND SHE LEAVES THE CLASSROOM, SHE WALKS OUT OF THE COLLEGE TO VISIT HER FRIEND.

LATER IN THE DAY TINA WAS AT HER APARTMENT WEARING HER WHITE NIKE T-SHIRT WITH A WHITE TRACKSUIT BOTTOM, SHE WALKS INTO THE KITCHEN BAREFOOT AS SHE WAS FEELING STRESS AND LOW ABOUT HER LOVE LIFE, BUT THERE WAS SOMETHING ELSE THAT WAS CAUSING HER A LOT OF PAIN AND SORROW SUDDENLY THERE'S A KNOCK ON THE DOOR, SHE LEAVES THE KITCHEN TO ANSWER THE DOOR AND IT WAS CATHY AND SHE SAYS TO HER "HI."

TINA SAYS TO CATHY "WHAT ARE YOU DOING HERE?"

CATHY SAYS "I'VE COME TO SEE YOU. CAN I COME IN."

TINA SAYS "YEAH SURE."

TINA LETS CATHY IN AND SHE SHUTS THE FRONT DOOR AND THEY BOTH LOOK AT EACH OTHER.

CATHY SAYS TO TINA "WHY HAVEN'T YOU COME TO CLASS?"

TINA SAYS "I HAVE FAMILY PROBLEMS."

CATHY SAYS "WELL YOU CAN TALK TO ME. I'M YOUR FRIEND."

TINA WALKS INTO THE LOUNGE AND SHE WANTED CATHY TO LEAVE

HER ALONE.

CATHY SAYS TO TINA "LET'S GO FOR A COFFEE. YOU DON'T HAVE TO TELL ME YOUR PROBLEMS. PLEASE LET ME TAKE YOU OUT."

TINA SAYS "LET ME GET MY TRAINERS FROM MY BEDROOM."

TINA LEAVES THE LOUNGE AND SHE GOES IN HER BEDROOM TO WEAR, HER NIKE WHITE TRAINERS AND CATHY WAITS FOR HER AT THE FRONT DOOR.


LATER IN THE DAY TINA AND CATHY WERE BOTH IN TOWN AND THEY WERE BOTH WALKING IN THE STREET, BOTH LOOKING STRESSED AND QUITE TO EACH OTHER AND THEY SEE A DYKE MARCH IN THE ROAD.

DYKE MARCH IS A GAY PRIDE, WHICH IS HELD IN MANY, CITES AROUND THE WORLD AND SAN FRANCISCO IS ONE OF THEM, TO CELEBRATE THE LESBIAN AND GAY COMMUNITY FOR THEIR RIGHTS.

CATHY AND TINA BOTH FIND OUT WHAT THE FUSS IS ABOUT AND SO, THEY BOTH WALK INTO THE MARCH HAVING NO IDEA OF WHAT IT WAS.

A 38-YEAR-OLD LESBIAN WOMAN WITH SHORT BLONDE HAIR AND BLUE EYES WEARING JEANS AND A BLACK T-SHIRT, WITH BLUE SANDALS WAS HOLDING SEVERAL FLOWER NECKLACES AND SHE GOES UP TO TINA AND CATHY.

THE WOMAN SAYS TO TINA AND CATHY "YOU MUST BE A COUPLE."

THE WOMAN PUTS A FLOWER NECKLACE ON TINA AND CATHY AND THEY BOTH STAND THERE LOOKING PUZZLED.

THE WOMAN SAYS TO TINA AND CATHY "GOD BLESS YOU BOTH."

THE WOMAN WALKS OFF TINA AND CATHY BOTH STAND THERE WHILE, MEN AND WOMEN WERE WALKING PASS THEM CELEBRATING THEIR LESBIAN AND GAY RIGHTS.

TINA SAYS TO CATHY "THAT WOMAN THINKS WE ARE A COUPLE."

CATHY AND TINA BOTH LAUGH AND GIGGLE WITH EACH OTHER ABOUT, THEM BEING A COUPLE AND THEY WALK IN THE MARCH TO SUPPORT THEM.

THE NEXT THING TINA WAS AT HER APARTMENT AND SHE WAS IN THE LOUNGE SAT ON THE SOFA, NEXT TO CATHY AND THEIR FLOWER NECKLACES WERE ON THE COFFEE TABLE.

CATHY SAYS TO TINA "I WILL SEE YOU IN CLASS TOMORROW."

TINA SAYS "NO I WON'T BE BACK FOR A LITTLE WHILE."

CATHY SAYS "OK. BUT YOU KNOW I'M ALWAYS HERE FOR YOU."

TINA SAYS "YOU SHOULD GO."

TINA WAS BEING DISTANCE TOWARDS CATHY SHE WAS HIDING HER LOVE FOR DAVID.

CATHY GETS UP FROM THE SOFA AND SHE LEAVES THE LOUNGE AND SHE WALKS TO THE FRONT DOOR.

TINA WAS SAT ON THE SOFA LIKE A DOLL AND SHE HEARS THE DOOR SHUT BY CATHY, SHE TAKES A DEEP SIGH AS SHE HAD HER OWN PERSONAL PROBLEMS, SHE WAS READY TO BREAK UP WITH DAVID.

WHY IS TINA HIDING FROM CATHY AND DAVID?

HAS TINA FALLEN IN LOVE WITH CATHY?

LATER THAT NIGHT DAVID WAS ROUND CATHY'S HOUSE AND THEY WERE BOTH IN THE GARDEN, IT WAS A CLOUDY GREY NIGHT AND THEY WERE BOTH STANDING, NEXT TO EACH OTHER FEELING THE LOVE AND HAPPINESS.

DAVID SAYS TO CATHY "I WANTED TO TELL YOU SOMETHING?"

CATHY HAD BEEN WAITING FOR THIS MOMENT TO COME AND DAVID SAYS TO HER "TINA IS MY GIRLFRIEND."

CATHY WAS HORRIFIED AND SHOCKED IT WAS LIKE HER LOVE AND FEELINGS FOR DAVID HAD BEEN CUT OF HER LIFE IN A SPLIT

SECOND.

DAVID SAYS TO CATHY "WELL SAY SOMETHING."

CATHY SAYS "I'M HAPPY FOR YOU."

CATHY DIDN'T WANT TO LOOK AT DAVID'S EYES, BECAUSE IT HAD HURT HER VERY DEEPLY IN HER HEART.

DAVID SAYS TO CATHY "LET'S GO INSIDE."

CATHY SAYS "OK."

DAVID TURNS AROUND AND HE GOES INSIDE THE HOUSE AND HE WALKS INTO THE LOUNGE, HE SITS ON THE SOFA WHILE CATHY WAS STANDING OUTSIDE IN THE GARDEN, SHE COULDN'T HELP BUT TO HAVE TEARS FLOWING DOWN FROM HER CHEEKS.

CATHY COULDN'T BELIEVE SHE FELL IN LOVE WITH THE WRONG PERSON, SHE FELT EMPTY IN HER LIFE AND IT SOON BECAME DULL AND LONELY AGAIN.

LOVE HAD NEVER LAST FOR TINA, CATHY AND DAVID IT HAD FADED AWAY IN THEIR LIVES.

WHO'S HEART WILL STOP BEATING FOR LOVE?

## CHAPTER SEVEN
### BROKEN HEARTS

THE SEASONS OF HEARTBREAKS HAD WALKED INTO CATHY, TINA AND DAVID'S LIFE.

HAS TINA BROKEN HER OWN HEART FOR HAVING DAVID AND CATHY IN HER LIFE?

IT WAS A TUESDAY AFTERNOON AND TINA WAS ROUND DAVID'S HOUSE AND THEY WERE BOTH IN THE LOUNGE BOTH SAT CLOSE NEXT TO EACH OTHER ON THE SOFA.

TINA LOOKED TENSE AND WORRIED AND SHE HAD SOMETHING TO SAY, BUT SHE WAS SCARED OF BREAKING DAVID'S HEART.

TINA LOOKS AT DAVID AND SHE SAYS TO HIM "I NEED TO TELL YOU SOMETHING. I HOPE YOU WILL UNDERSTAND."

DAVID LOOKS AT TINA AND SHE MOVES AWAY FROM HIM WITH A BRAVE HEART AND SHE SAYS TO HIM "I HAVE HIV."

DAVID WAS HORRIFIED AND HE WAS SPEECHLESS AND TINA WAS LOOKING SCARED, SHE WAS IN PAIN BECAUSE OF HER ILLNESS AND SHE SAYS TO HIM "I'M SORRY I KNOW I CAN NOT BE WITH YOU."

DAVID SAYS "NOW I KNOW WHY YOU WOULDN'T WANT TO HAVE SEX WITH ME."

DAVID LOOKS AT TINA AND HE GOES CLOSER TO HER AND HE TOUCHES HER FACE, THEY BOTH LOOK AT EACH OTHER WITH PAIN AND HURT AND HE SAYS TO HER "I LOVE YOU."

DAVID AND TINA BOTH CRY FOR EACH OTHER AND THEY HOLD ON TO EACH OTHER LIKE A ROCK.

TINA SAYS TO DAVID "I HAVE TO BREAK UP WITH YOU. I NEED

TO BE ON MY OWN."

DAVID SAYS "I'M HERE FOR YOU."

TINA SAYS "I'M DIEING AND I KNOW THERE'S SOMEONE WHO WANTS TO BE WITH YOU."

TINA MOVES AWAY FROM DAVID AND SHE GETS UP FROM THE SOFA AND SHE LEAVES THE LOUNGE, SHE GOES TO OPEN THE FRONT DOOR AND SHE WALKS OUT AND SHE SHUTS THE DOOR, SHE CRIES FOR BREAKING DAVID'S HEART AND SHE TAKES A MOURNFUL CRY.

WILL DAVID TAKE CARE OF TINA OR, WILL HE HAVE A CRUEL HEART TO LEAVE HER TO SUFFER ALONE?

LATER IN THE DAY IT WAS RAINING AND TINA WAS WALKING ALONG THE SANDY BEACH ALONE, SHE WAS FEELING COLD AND WET AS SHE WISHED THAT SHE COULD THROW HER ILLNESS INTO THE DEEP SEA, SO SHE COULD HAVE A HAPPY LIFE AND SHE CRIES AS SHE WAS WALKING.

CATHY WAS AT HOME STANDING OUTSIDE IN THE GARDEN FEELING THE RAIN FALL ON HER AND SHE CROSSES HER ARMS, SHE WAS ANGRY AND UPSET WITH HERSELF FOR FALLING IN LOVE AGAIN AND SHE LOOKS UP, AT THE CLOUDY GREY SKY AND SHE COULD SEE THE RAIN FALLING ON HER FACE AND SHE CRIES.

LATER THAT NIGHT TINA WAS AT HER APARTMENT IN HER BEDROOM LYING ON THE BED, SHE WAS THINKING ABOUT HER LIFE WITHOUT DAVID AND CATHY AND SHE HAS TEARS IN HER EYES.

DAVID WAS AT HOME UPSTAIRS IN HIS ROOM LYING ON THE BED THINKING ABOUT TINA'S LIFE AND HER ILLNESS, HE SITS UP FROM THE BED AND HE TAKES A DEEP SIGH OF SORROW, HE RUNS HIS HANDS THREW HIS SHORT BROWN HAIR AND HE CRIES IN SADNESS.

CATHY WAS AT HOME UPSTAIRS IN HER BEDROOM LYING ON THE BED

AND SHE HAD THE PILLOW CLOSE TO HER CHEST, AS SHE CRIES QUIETLY SO HER PARENTS, COULD NOT HEAR HER PAIN AND SORROW FOR THE ONE SHE LOVED.

IT WAS A SAD AND UNHAPPY NIGHT IN SAN FRANCISCO AS THREE PEOPLE WERE LONGING FOR LOVE, HOPE AND HAPPINESS BUT IT HAD BEEN TAKEN AWAY FROM THEM.

COULD IT BE A HAPPY ENDING FOR ONE OF THEM?

THE NEXT MORNING DAVID WAS ROUND TINA'S PLACE AND THEY WERE IN THE LOUNGE, HE WAS SAT ON THE SOFA AND SHE WAS STANDING NEAR THE COFFEE TABLE.

DAVID SAYS TO TINA "I LOVE YOU AND I WON'T LET YOU GO."

TINA SAYS "YOU HAVE TO STOP LOVING ME. I ONLY HAVE A SHORT TIME TO BE IN THIS LIFE."

TINA HAD TEARS IN HER EYES AND SHE SAYS TO DAVID "I KNOW THAT CATHY LOVES YOU AND SHE WANTS TO BE WITH YOU."

TINA GOES UP TO DAVID AND SHE HOLDS HIS HAND, THEY WERE BOTH LOOKING AT EACH OTHER FOR A WAY OUT IN THEIR DIFFICULT LIVES.

TINA SAYS TO DAVID "MOVE ON WITH YOUR LIFE. DO THIS FOR ME. PLEASE."

DAVID WAS LOOKING AT TINA AND HE HAD TEARS IN HIS EYES, HE GETS UP FROM SOFA WHILE HOLDING ON TO HER HAND, HE GIVES HER A WARM HUG TO EASE THE PAIN THEY BOTH HAD FOR EACH OTHER.

TINA WAS SCARED OF HER LIFE AND DAVID WAS ALWAYS THERE TO SUPPORT AND COMFORT HER.

WILL CATHY HOLD ON TO HER LOVE OR MOVE FAR AWAY FROM DAVID AND TINA?

LATER IN THE DAY TINA WAS AT HER APARTMENT WITH DAVID AND
THEY WERE BOTH SAT AT THE DINNER TABLE, DRINKING A CUP
EACH OF WARM TEA AS SHE SITS THERE SHE WAS THINKING ABOUT
CATHY, SHE WAS MISSING HER AND IT WAS HURTING HER FOR NOT
BEING WITH HER DEAREST FRIEND.

## Chapter Eight
### Love Again

It was October 31ˢᵗ the eve of All Saints Day it's popular with children in the UK, US and Canada. The children dress up as witches or ghosts and play traditional games, or go from door to door asking for sweets and saying trick or treat.

Cathy was at home and she was in the kitchen and she was holding a glass of water, she was watching her mum cutting a small round circle with a small sharp knife on a small fat pumpkin.

Cathy stands there and she wasn't impressed about Halloween and Susan says to her "Are you going to help me this evening?"

Cathy says "No I don't like Halloween."

Susan says "Of course you do. Last month you told me that you were happy to help me and you couldn't wait for Halloween."

Cathy was looking angry and it was causing her stress and says quietly "Halloween sucks."

Cathy walks out of the kitchen holding on to her glass of water and she goes into the lounge, looking moody and unhappy and she sits on the sofa, drinking her glass of water to cool her down.

Tina was at her apartment in the lounge sat on the sofa watching Friday the 13ᵀᴴ on T.V, eating a small bowl of salted popcorn.

LATER THAT AFTERNOON DAVID WAS ROUND TINA'S PLACE AND THEY WERE BOTH SAT AT THE DINNER TABLE, BOTH HOLDING ON TO EACH OTHER'S HAND FOR COMFORT AND SUPPORT FOR ONE ANOTHER.
TINA SAYS TO DAVID "HAVE YOU SPOKEN TO CATHY?"
DAVID SAYS "I'VE CALLED HER BUT SHE SAYS THAT SHE IS BUSY."
TINA SAYS "YOU NEED TO SEE CATHY AND BE THERE FOR HER. I KNOW YOU WILL FALL IN LOVE AGAIN."
DAVID SAYS "I DON'T THINK I CAN FALL IN LOVE AGAIN."
TINA SAYS "GO AND SEE CATHY THIS EVENING AND TRY TO TALK TO HER."

WILL DAVID TAKE ON TINA'S ADVICE?

LATER THAT EVENING CATHY WAS AT HOME AND SHE WAS IN THE LOUNGE LYING ON THE SOFA, LOOKING TIRED AND UPSET FROM THE PAIN AND SADNESS SHE HAD IN HER LIFE, SUDDENLY THE DOOR BELL RINGS AND SHE GETS UP FROM THE SOFA, SHE LEAVES THE LOUNGE TO ANSWER THE DOOR, IT WAS DAVID AND HE SMILES AT HER AND SHE WAS SHOCKED TO SEE HIM STANDING THERE.
CATHY SAYS TO DAVID "WHAT ARE YOU DOING HERE?"
DAVID SAYS TO CATHY "I'VE COME TO SEE YOU."
CATHY WASN'T IN A HAPPY MOOD TO SEEING DAVID AND TALKING TO HIM, AS HE HAD NO LOVE INTEREST WITH HER.
CATHY SAYS TO DAVID "COME IN."
CATHY LET'S DAVID IN THE HOUSE AND SHE SHUTS THE FRONT DOOR.
THE NEXT THING CATHY AND DAVID WERE BOTH IN THE KITCHEN STANDING FAR AWAY FROM EACH OTHER, HE KEPT HIS PROMISE FROM TINA THAT HE WOULD TRY AND MOVE ON WITH HIS LIFE AND TO FALL IN LOVE AGAIN, SHE STANDS THERE KNOWING THAT SHE HAD TO MOVE ON WITH HER LIFE, HAVING TO ACCEPT THAT NO

ONE WOULD LOVE HER.

DAVID SAYS TO CATHY "HAVE I UPSET YOU."

CATHY SAYS "NO I'M JUST STRESSED WITH WORK."

DAVID SAYS "ARE WE STILL FRIENDS."

CATHY SAYS "YEAH."

DAVID GOES UP TO CATHY AND SHE LOOKS AT HIM NOT KNOWING WHAT TO SAY TO HIM AND HE GIVES HER A HUG.

CATHY HOLDS DAVID IN HER ARMS AND SHE COULD FEEL THE WARMTH AND LOVE, SHE HAD FOR HIM AND THEY BOTH LOOK AT EACH OTHER.

CATHY SAYS TO DAVID "SO HOW IS TINA?"

DAVID SAYS "SHE'S ALRIGHT."

CATHY SAYS "I GUESS YOU WILL BE MOVING IN WITH HER."

DAVID SAYS "NO. ME AND TINA HAVE BROKEN UP."

CATHY WAS SHOCKED SHE COULDN'T UNDERSTAND WHY AND SHE SAYS TO DAVID "WHAT HAPPENED?"

DAVID SAYS "THERE WAS A AGE GAP BETWEEN ME AND TINA."

CATHY THOUGHT TINA WAS BEING UNREASONABLE AND SHE DIDN'T LIKE HER AND SHE SAYS TO DAVID "SHE'S NOTHING SPECIAL."

DAVID SAYS "BUT YOU ARE."

CATHY AND DAVID BOTH LOOK AT EACH OTHER AND HE SAYS TO HER "SHALL WE GO FOR LUNCH TOMORROW?"

CATHY SAYS "OK."

DAVID SMILES AT CATHY AND SHE SAYS TO HIM "WOULD YOU LIKE A CUP OF COFFEE."

DAVID SAYS "YES PLEASE."

CATHY PUTS THE KETTLE ON AND SHE OPENS THE TOP CUPBOARD DRAW TO GET A EMPTY CUP OUT AND DAVID GETS HIS MOBILE OUT OF HIS JEANS POCKET TO TEXT TINA.

TINA WAS AT HER APARTMENT STANDING OUTSIDE THE TERRACE WATCHING A GROUP OF TEN YEAR OLDS, WEARING SCARY MASKS AND SUITS HOLDING SMALL BAGS OF SWEETS AND CHOCOLATES, STANDING

IN THE STREET LOOKING HAPPY AND CHEERFUL.

TINA WAS TAKING SOME FRESH AIR AND SHE HEARS HER MOBILE BUZZING INSIDE, SHE GOES INSIDE TO THE DINNER TABLE, TO SEE HER PHONE AND IT WAS A TEXT MESSAGE FROM DAVID ASKING IF SHE WAS OK.

TINA KNEW THAT DAVID WAS BY HER SIDE AND HE KNEW HER ILLNESS, BUT IT WAS HURTING HER TO KEEP HER SECRET AWAY FROM CATHY.

HOW LONG WILL TINA HIDE HER ILLNESS AWAY FROM CATHY?

THE NEXT DAY CATHY AND DAVID WERE BOTH IN TOWN WALKING AT MARKET STREET, IT'S THE FERRY BUILDING A PUBLIC SPACE OF A FOOD HALL, RESTAURANTS AND A FARMERS MARKET THEY WERE BOTH LOOKING AT THE FRUIT & VEG, THEY BROUGHT A RED APPLE EACH TO EAT.

TINA WAS AT HER APARTMENT AND SHE WAS SAT AT THE DINNER TABLE PUTTING HER EXERCISE BOOKS, IN HER BLACK RUCKSACK THAT SHE WAS GOING TO TAKE TOMORROW FOR LESSON.

LATER THAT EVENING CATHY AND DAVID WERE BOTH WALKING TO HER HOUSE, THEY GO TO THE FRONT DOOR AND HE SAYS TO HER "I'M NOT GOING INSIDE."

CATHY SAYS "WHY?"

DAVID SAYS "BECAUSE I NEED TO MAKE A FEW CALLS ABOUT WORK."

CATHY SAYS "OK SO I'LL SEE YOU TOMORROW."

DAVID SAYS "YES I'LL SEE YOU TOMORROW EVENING."

DAVID GIVES CATHY A KISS ON THE CHEEK AND HE TURNS AROUND AND HE WALKS OFF, SHE KNOCKS ON THE DOOR STANDING THERE FOR 2 MINUTES AND SUSAN OPENS THE FRONT DOOR.

SUSAN SAYS TO CATHY "HIYA."

CATHY SAYS "HI MUM."

CATHY WALKS GOES INSIDE THE HOUSE AND SUSAN SHUTS THE FRONT DOOR AND THEY BOTH LOOK AT EACH OTHER.

SUSAN SAYS TO CATHY "SO HOW WAS YOUR DAY?"

CATHY SAYS "IT WAS ALRIGHT."

SUSAN SAYS "IS DAVID YOUR BOYFRIEND?"

CATHY SAYS "NO WERE FRIENDS. GOOD FRIENDS."

SUSAN SMILES AT CATHY AND SHE WAS PLEASED TO SEE HER DAUGHTER HAPPY AGAIN, SHE GOES TO THE LOUNGE TO SIT ON THE SOFA.

CATHY STANDS NEAR THE FRONT DOOR AND SHE COULDN'T UNDERSTAND WHY TINA BROKE UP WITH DAVID, IT HAD MADE HER FEEL ANGRY AND UPSET AND SHE TAKES A DEEP SIGH.

WILL CATHY AND TINA HAVE A BIG ARGUMENT OR, WILL THEY BOTH KEEP THEIR DISTANCE AWAY FROM EACH OTHER?


THE NEXT MORNING TINA WAS AT THE COLLEGE AND SHE WAS HOLDING HER BLACK RUCKSACK, IN HER HAND FEELING HAPPY TO BE THERE AND TO SEE CATHY.

THE NEXT THING TINA WAS IN THE CLASSROOM AND SHE WAS SAT AT HER DESK WITH 13 OTHER STUDENTS, CATHY WALKS IN AND THEY BOTH LOOK AT EACH OTHER, LIKE A BATTLE WAS GOING TO HAPPEN ANY MINUTE BETWEEN THE TWO.

TINA SAYS TO CATHY "HI MADAM."

CATHY IGNORES TINA AND SHE WALKS TO THE FRONT OF THE DESK TO PICK UP, 14 TEXTBOOKS ABOUT ENGLISH AND SHE GIVES THEM TO THE STUDENTS.

CATHY SLAMS THE TEXTBOOK ON TINA'S DESK AND SHE JUMPS UP IN HER CHAIR WITH A FRIGHT.

WHILE TINA WAS ATTENDING HER LESSONS FOR FOUR WEEKS CATHY WOULD GIVE HER ATTITUDE.


HOW LONG WILL TINA KEEP QUITE FROM CATHY?

As the days were passing by David would meet Cathy, he would make her laugh and bring happiness into her life.

Tina was in college and she was standing near her locker, she sees Cathy walking out of the classroom she could see, her happiness and love back into her friend's life and she was pleased.

But Tina felt alone and empty in her life and she was yearning for a longer life, she leans back on her locker and she takes sigh.

Tina wanted to be Cathy's friend but they would, both keep away from each other in break and lunch time.

Later that evening Cathy was at home and she was outside in the garden with David, she was holding a bunch of red roses that he had brought for her.

David says to Cathy "Will you marry me."

Cathy and David both look at each other and they both could feel the love for each other and she says to him "Yes I will marry you."

David and Cathy give each other a quick hug, they both gaze into each other's eyes and they have a passionate kiss.

Will San Francisco fill the colours of Cathy and David's heart with love?

Leaving Tina's love blowing far away from her to the gateway of heavens.

## Chapter Nine
## <u>The Truth Hurts</u>

It's a new month in November and it was a cold and windy day, Tina walks out of the hospital as her face was looking stressed and ill, her mobile rings in her black jacket pocket and she takes it out to answer, the call and it was David.

David says "Hi Tina"

Tina says over the phone "Hiya."

David says "Are you alright."

Tina says "Yes I'm fine."

David says "I have good news to tell you. I'm engaged."

Tina says "Congratulations. Well done David."

David says "Thanks. I'll see you later take care. Bye Tina."

Tina says "Bye David."

Tina takes her mobile away from her ear and she puts it in her jacket pocket, she was feeling down and sad for not telling Cathy the truth about her, she had tears in her eyes.

Will Tina have enough time to tell Cathy the truth?

Later in the day Tina was at college in the classroom on her own waiting for Cathy, so she could have a chance to talk to her.

Cathy walks out of the staff room looking happy and cheerful and she goes to her classroom, she sees Tina

STANDING THERE WAITING FOR HER.

CATHY LOOKED ANGRY SEEING TINA AND THEY BOTH LOOK AT EACH OTHER LIKE THEY WERE READY FOR A FIGHT.

CATHY SAYS TO TINA "WHAT ARE YOU DOING HERE?"

TINA SAYS "I NEED TO TALK TO YOU."

TINA SEES CATHY'S DIAMOND RING ON HER LEFT HAND AND SHE WAS PLEASED FOR HER.

CATHY SAYS TO TINA "I HAVE NOTHING TO SAY TO YOU."

TINA SAYS "I WANT US TO BE FRIENDS."

CATHY GETS ANGRY AND FRUSTRATED WITH TINA AND SHE SHUTS THE DOOR, SO KNOW ONE IN THE COLLEGE COULD HEAR THERE ARGUING.

CATHY SAYS TO TINA "HOW CAN WE BE FRIENDS. YOU'RE A MEAN GIRL. YOU BROKE DAVID'S HEART."

TINA SAYS "I HAD TO. YOU WON'T UNDERSTAND."

CATHY SHOUTS AT TINA "**UNDERSTAND! YOU'RE A BITCH! I HATE YOU!**"

TINA WAS SHOCKED AND SHE HAD NO CHOICE BUT TO TELL CATHY THE TRUTH.

TINA SHOUTS AT CATHY "**I'M DYING!** I HAVE **HIV.** AND I HAVE LITTLE TIME LEFT IN THIS LIFE TO BE WITH YOU AND DAVID."

CATHY LOOKS AT TINA AND SHE WAS HORRIFIED, OF WHAT SHE HAD SAID TO HER AND SHE HAD TEARS IN HER EYES.

CATHY SAYS "SO HOW ABOUT DAVID. HAS HE GOT."

TINA SAYS "NO. DAVID AND ME DIDN'T HAVE SEX BUT ALL I WANTED WAS TO BE LOVED. I WANTED TO FALL IN LOVE."

TINA CRIES HER HEART OUT AND CATHY QUICKLY GOES UP TO HER AND SHE HOLDS HER TIGHT IN HER ARMS.

CATHY SAYS TO TINA "WHY DIDN'T YOU TELL ME."

CATHY AND TINA BOTH LOOK AT EACH OTHER AND THEY CRY TOGETHER.

CATHY SAYS TO TINA "I DON'T WANT YOU TO GO."
TINA SAYS "I WAS MEANT TO HAVE A SHORT LIFE."
CATHY HOLDS TINA CLOSE TO HER SO SHE COULD FEEL HER PAIN,
SORROW AND HURT IN HER HEART.
CATHY SAYS TO TINA "I'M GOING TO LOOK AFTER YOU."
TINA CRIES ON CATHY'S SHOULDER AND SHE SAYS TO HER
"THANK YOU."
AS TWO BROKEN HEARTS WERE HOLDING ON TO EACH OTHER FOR
DEAR LIFE OUTSIDE THE COLLEGE, IT WAS VERY COLD AND IT
STARTS TO SNOW, AS IT WAS A NEW BEGINNING OF DEATH AND
SADNESS FOR THEM.

LATER THAT NIGHT CATHY WAS AT HOME IN THE LOUNGE AND SHE
WAS STANDING NEAR THE FIREPLACE, SHE WAS LOOKING AT HER
DIAMOND RING ON HER FINGER SHE WAS UPSET, OF TINA'S
ILLNESS AND HER PAIN AND SHE TAKES A DEEP SIGH.
TINA WAS AT HER APARTMENT AND SHE WAS IN THE LOUNGE LYING
ON THE SOFA, SHE HAD THE CUSHION CLOSE TO HER CHEST AND
SHE WAS CRYING, OF HER ILLNESS AND HER LOVE FOR DAVID AND
LOSING HER FRIENDSHIP WITH CATHY.

AS THE NIGHT WAS COLD AND WINDY IT WAS STILL SNOWING IN
SAN FRANCISCO AS ONE-GIRL'S DREAMS WAS SOON GOING TO
DISAPPEAR INTO THE DARKNESS.
THE NEXT MORNING CATHY WAS ROUND TINA'S PLACE AND THEY
WERE BOTH IN THE LOUNGE, SAT NEXT TO EACH OTHER ON THE
SOFA HOLDING EACH OTHER'S HAND FOR LOVE AND SUPPORT.
CATHY SAYS TO TINA "I'M ALWAYS HERE FOR YOU. WEATHER
ITS DAY OR NIGHT. YOU'RE MY DEAREST FRIEND."
TINA LEANS ON CATHY'S SHOULDER AND SHE HAD TEARS IN HER
EYES.
TINA SAYS TO CATHY "PROMISE ME THAT WHEN I AM GONE THAT

YOU WON'T BE ON YOUR OWN."

CATHY SITS THERE WITH TINA CRYING ON HER SHOULDER SHE ALREADY, HAS A BROKEN HEART FOR SAYING GOODBYE TO HER FRIEND.

TINA DIDN'T WANT CATHY TO BE ON HER OWN AND TO SUFFER IN SILENCE.

HAS TINA MADE THE RIGHT DECISION BY TELLING CATHY THE TRUTH?

WILL DAVID HAVE A BROKEN HEART AGAIN?

# CHAPTER TEN
## THE LAST MOMENT

AS THE SUN WAS GOING DOWN IN SNOWY SAN FRANCISCO IT SOON BECAME DULL, COLD AND WINDY AS A GIRL'S LIFE, LOVE AND HAPPINESS WAS COMING TO AN END.

IT WAS THE MONTH OF DECEMBER AND EVERYONE IN TOWN WAS CELEBRATING CHRISTMAS WITH LOVE, JOY AND HAPPINESS BUT THERE WAS ONE PERSON WHO WAS LEAVING, THAT BEHIND AND WAS GOING TO THE HEAVENS TO BE WITH THE ANGELS.

CATHY WAS ROUND DAVID'S HOUSE AND THEY WERE IN THE LOUNGE BOTH STANDING NEAR THE FIREPLACE, SHE WAS LOOKING STRESSED AND UPSET ABOUT SOMETHING.
CATHY TAKES HER DIAMOND RING OFF HER LEFT HAND AND SHE SAYS TO DAVID "I'M BREAKING UP WITH YOU."
DAVID IS SHOCKED AND HE PANIC, IT WAS LIKE HIS HEART HAD STOP BEATING FOR LOVE AND HE SAYS TO HER "I LOVE YOU AND I WANT TO SPEND THE REST OF MY LIFE WITH YOU."
CATHY SAYS "I CAN'T BECAUSE I'M NOT READY TO MARRY YOU."
DAVID SAYS "OK I WILL WAIT. I KNOW YOUR UPSET ABOUT TINA."
CATHY CRIES HEARING TINA'S NAME AND SHE GIVES THE DIAMOND RING, TO DAVID AND HE TAKES IT FROM HER AND HE SAYS TO HER "I'LL BE WAITING FOR YOU."
CATHY LEAVES THE LOUNGE NOT SAYING A WORD AND SHE GOES TO THE FRONT DOOR, DAVID WAS STANDING NEAR THE FIREPLACE

LOOKING AT THE DIAMOND RING, HE HEARS THE DOOR SHUT AND HE TAKES A SIGH OF PAIN, REGRET AND HURT HE HAD IN HIS LIFE. CATHY WAS OUTSIDE DAVID'S HOUSE AND SHE WALKS IN THE STREET FEELING COLD AND THE SNOW, FALLING ON HER SHE CROSSES HER ARMS AS SHE TRIES TO GET AWAY, FROM THE PAIN AND SADNESS SHE HAD IN HER LIFE BUT IT WAS THERE IN HER HEART.

AS THE DAYS WERE PASSING BY IN THE MONTH OF DECEMBER IT WAS THE 24TH AND TINA WAS IN HOSPITAL, IN THE ROOM LYING ON THE BED FIGHTING FOR HER LAST BREATH OF LIFE, CATHY AND DAVID WERE BOTH SAT BY HER HOLDING HER HAND.
TINA LOOKS AT CATHY AND DAVID AND HER TIME HAD COME HER HEART WOULD STOP ANY MINUTE, TO STOP BEATING AND SHE SHUTS HER EYES KNOWING HER TIME HAD COME TO SAY GOODBYE.
CATHY AND DAVID BOTH CRY FOR TINA AS HER LIFE, HAD ENDED AND THEY HAD LOST A LOVED ONE CLOSE TO THEIR HEART.

CATHY TAKES A MOURNFUL CRY AS SHE SITS NEAR TINA HOLDING ON TO HER HAND, AS SHE COULD NOT FEEL ANY LIFE AND SHE KISSES IT.

AS THE EVENING WAS A SAD AND DEVASTATING MOMENT FOR TWO PEOPLE, IT WAS SNOWING HEAVILY IN SAN FRANCISCO AS IT WAS MISSING THE LIFE AND SOUL OF TINA.

WHAT WILL HAPPEN TO CATHY AND DAVID'S LOVE FOR EACH OTHER?

WILL THEY BOTH END UP BEING TOGETHER?

TWO YEARS HAD PASSED AND IT WAS THE MONTH OF JUNE AND

CATHY WOULD BE IN COLLEGE, SHE WOULD KEEP TINA'S HOMEWORK WITH HER, SOMETIMES SHE WOULD TELL HER GROUP ABOUT HER DEAREST FRIEND.

CATHY WAS MISSING TINA VERY DEEPLY BEING IN COLLEGE SHE LEAVES ALONE WITH AN EMPTY HEART.

LATER THAT AFTERNOON CATHY WAS AT THE GRAVEYARD AND SHE HAD PLACED A BUNCH OF YELLOW FLOWERS, ON TINA'S GRAVE AS SHE STANDS THERE SHE TAKES A DEEP SIGH, AS SHE FELT WEAK AND ILL BEING IN A PLACE OF DEATH.

CATHY TURNS AROUND AND SHE WALKS OFF AND SHE LEAVES THE GRAVEYARD ALONE, SUDDENLY THE WIND BLOWS TO HER LIKE TINA WAS THERE WITH HER.

LATER THAT EVENING CATHY WAS AT HOME AND SHE WAS SAT AT THE DINNER TABLE STARING AT TINA'S HOMEWORK BOOK, SUSAN WALKS OUT OF THE KITCHEN HOLDING A CUP OF HOT CHOCOLATE, SHE GOES TO SIT NEXT TO HER DAUGHTER AND SHE PUTS THE CUP ON THE TABLE.

SUSAN SAYS TO CATHY "I'VE MADE YOU A CUP OF HOT CHOCOLATE FOR YOU."

CATHY SAYS "I DON'T WANT IT. YOU HAVE IT."

SUSAN TOUCHES CATHY'S HAIR AND SHE SAYS TO HER "I KNOW YOUR MISSING TINA AND I KNOW IT IS HURTING YOU A LOT. YOU CAN TALK TO ME."

CATHY SAYS "THERE'S NO POINT OF TALKING. YOU CAN'T HELP ME. NO ONE CAN."

CATHY HAD TEARS FLOWING DOWN FROM HER CHEEKS AND SUSAN TOUCHES HER FACE, SHE COULDN'T BEAR SEEING HER DAUGHTER'S PAIN AND SORROW.

SUSAN SAYS TO CATHY "YOU HAVE TO BE STRONG."

CATHY SAYS "I DON'T THINK I CAN."

CATHY HAD NO ONE AND SHE DIDN'T MAKE ANY FRIENDS SHE

DIDN'T TALK TO HER PARENTS, ABOUT HER LIFE OR HER PROBLEMS, SHE WOULD BE ON HER OWN.

WILL CATHY GET OVER TINA'S DEATH AND BE HAPPY AGAIN?

OR WILL IT DESTROY HER LIFE?

## Chapter Eleven
## <u>Old Self</u>

It was a Monday afternoon and it was a warm sunny day in San Francisco, it wanted to give a little bit of love and happiness to Cathy, but she wasn't taking it she carried the dull and darkness, with her which wasn't letting her go in her life.

Cathy was at her quiet neighbourhood walking in the street looking down and depressed, when she sees David's blue BMW car parked outside her house.
David walks out of Matthew's house and they both looked worried and stressed about Cathy's problems.
David says to Matthew "Could you tell Cathy to call me."
Matthew says "Don't worry I'll tell her."
David says "Thanks bye."
Matthew says "Bye David."
David and Matthew both see Cathy walking towards the driveway and they were pleased to see her.
Cathy says to David "Hello."
David says to Cathy "Hi."
Cathy goes up to David wanting to know why he had come to see her, she wasn't happy to see him and her father could see that.
Matthew says to Cathy and David "I'll leave you both to it."
Matthew goes back inside the house leaving the front door

HALF OPEN, SO HIM AND SUSAN CAN HEAR THERE DAUGHTER'S PROBLEMS AND IF THEY, COULD BOTH HELP HER HAVE A HAPPY LIFE.

DAVID AND CATHY WERE BOTH STANDING NEAR THE FRONT DOOR AND HE WAS CONCERN ABOUT HER AND HE SAYS TO HER "YOU HAVEN'T CALLED ME FOR THE PAST YEAR. AND WHENEVER I COME ROUND YOUR ALWAYS OUT."

CATHY DIDN'T WANT DAVID TO BE IN HER LIFE AS SHE FELT, HAPPY BEING ALONE IN HER WORLD SHE TAKES A SIGH.

CATHY SAYS TO DAVID "I WANT TO BE ON MY OWN."

DAVID SAYS "YOU CAN'T LIVE LIKE THAT. YOU NEED PEOPLE IN YOUR LIFE."

DAVID STILL HAD FEELINGS FOR CATHY AND HE KNEW IT WOULD TAKE TIME FOR THEM, TO BE TOGETHER AS IT WAS A GREAT LOST FOR THE TWO OF THEM TO LOSE TINA.

DAVID SAYS TO CATHY "I WANT YOU TO COME ROUND MY PLACE. AND DON'T SAY NO."

CATHY WASN'T INTERESTED IN GOING ROUND DAVID'S HOUSE AND SHE HAD NO CHOICE BUT TO SAY YES TO HIM.

CATHY SAYS TO DAVID "OK FINE. I'LL SEE YOU TOMORROW."

DAVID SMILES AT CATHY AND HE HOLDS HER HAND, TO SHOW THAT HE CARED FOR HER AND HE SAYS TO HER "I'LL PICK YOU UP TOMORROW AFTERNOON."

DAVID LET GOES OF CATHY'S HAND AND HE WALKS TO HIS CAR AND SHE TURNS AROUND, TO PUSH THE FRONT DOOR SO SHE CAN WALK INSIDE, THE HOUSE AND SHE SHUTS THE DOOR.

MATTHEW AND SUSAN WERE BOTH IN THE KITCHEN AND THEY HEAR CATHY, RUNNING UPSTAIRS AND THEY HEAR HER BEDROOM DOOR SLAM.

SUSAN AND MATTHEW WERE BOTH STANDING NEAR THE KITCHEN TABLE, LOOKING WORRIED ABOUT THEIR DAUGHTER'S BEHAVIOUR.

SUSAN SAYS TO MATTHEW "DO YOU THINK I SHOULD TALK TO

CATHY?"

MATTHEW SAYS "I THINK IT'S BEST IF WE LEAVE HER ALONE
FOR A LITTLE WHILE."

SUSAN WAS UPSET FOR BEING HELPLESS AND SHE COULDN'T BEAR
SEEING HER DAUGHTER'S GRIEF, MATTHEW HOLDS HIS WIFE FOR
COMFORT, AS THEY BOTH FEEL UNHAPPY.


HOW LONG WILL CATHY GRIEVE FOR HER LOST FRIEND TINA?


THE NEXT DAY CATHY WAS ROUND DAVID'S HOUSE AND THEY WERE
BOTH SAT AT THE DINNER TABLE, THEY WERE BOTH QUIET WITH
EACH OTHER.

DAVID COULDN'T KEEP QUIET FOR ANY LONGER AND HE SAYS TO
CATHY "WOULD YOU LIKE TO STAY WITH ME FOR THE WEEKEND?"

CATHY LOOKS AT DAVID AND SHE DIDN'T WANT TO SPEND TIME
WITH HIM, AS SHE KNEW THAT WOULD BRING HER HAPPINESS AND
LOVE AND THAT WAS SCARING HER.

CATHY SAYS TO DAVID "NO. I NEED TIME TO MYSELF."

DAVID SAYS "YOU NEED TO SPEND TIME WITH YOUR FRIEND. AND
YOU'RE SCARED OF BEING HAPPY."

CATHY KNEW THAT DAVID WAS RIGHT ABOUT HER AND SHE GETS
EMOTIONAL AND HE SAYS TO HER "WILL YOU STAY."

CATHY SITS THERE IN HER CHAIR QUICKLY DECIDING, WHAT TO DO
AND SHE GIVES AN ANSWER TO DAVID.

CATHY SAYS TO DAVID "OK I WILL STAY WITH YOU FOR THE
WEEKEND."

DAVID WAS PLEASED THAT CATHY AGREED TO STAY WITH HIM FOR
THE WEEKEND AND HE TOUCHES HER FACE.


WILL DAVID AND CATHY MAKE ANOTHER GO IN THERE
RELATIONSHIP?

OR WILL IT BE JUST BE A GOOD FRIENDSHIP BETWEEN THE TWO?

IT WAS THE WEEKEND AND CATHY WAS ROUND DAVID'S HOUSE AND SHE WAS UPSTAIRS IN THE BEDROOM, SHE HAD HER SMALL BLACK SUITCASE WITH CLOTHES AND A FEW SHOES, WHICH WERE ON THE FLOOR NEAR THE SINGLE BED.

DAVID SHOUTS FROM DOWNSTAIRS "CATHY!"

CATHY LEAVES THE BEDROOM AND SHE GOES DOWNSTAIRS AND WALKS INTO THE LOUNGE, WHERE DAVID HAD DINNER READY ON THE TABLE WITH TWO GLASSES OF RED WINE.

CATHY WAS SURPRISED AND SHE SAYS TO DAVID "YOU'VE MADE DINNER."

DAVID SAYS "YES. IT'S ROAST CHICKEN WITH SALAD."

CATHY GOES TO THE TABLE TO SIT DOWN AND DAVID, SITS NEXT TO HER AND THEY BOTH ATE THEIR MEAL TOGETHER.

DAVID WANTED A CHANCE TO BE IN CATHY'S LIFE AND TO MAKE HER HAPPY.

LATER THAT EVENING DAVID AND CATHY WERE BOTH IN THE LOUNGE, SAT NEXT TO EACH OTHER ON THE SOFA WATCHING A FILM CALLED WEREWOLF.

CATHY GOES CLOSER TO DAVID AND SHE LEANS, ON HIS SHOULDER TO SHOW THAT SHE CARED FOR HIM.

COULD THIS BE THE MOMENT DAVID HAS BEEN WAITING FOR?

LATER THAT NIGHT DAVID WAS UPSTAIRS AND HE WAS IN HIS ROOM, CATHY WALKS UPSTAIRS AND SHE SEES HIM IN HIS BEDROOM.

CATHY GOES TO DAVID'S ROOM AND THEY BOTH LOOK AT EACH OTHER AND SHE SAYS TO HIM "GOODNIGHT."

DAVID SAYS TO CATHY "GOODNIGHT."

CATHY GOES UP TO DAVID AND SHE GIVES HIM A KISS ON THE
CHEEK AND THEY BOTH GAZE INTO EACH OTHER'S EYES, THEY BOTH
FELT AN INTENSE FEELING FOR ONE ANOTHER AND THEY HAVE A
PASSIONATE KISS, THEY SLOWLY BOTH WALK BACK TO LIE ON THE
BED AS THEY WERE BOTH HOLDING ON TO EACH OTHER.

HAS CATHY FINALLY FALLEN IN LOVE AGAIN?

THE NEXT MORNING CATHY WAS IN DAVID'S BED WITH THE DUVET
ON HER, SHE WAS CRYING QUIETLY BECAUSE SHE HAD NO LOVE
FOR HIM.
DAVID WAS DOWNSTAIRS WEARING A BLACK T-SHIRT WITH A BLACK
TRACKSUIT BOTTOM AND HE WAS IN THE KITCHEN, MAKING TWO
FRIED EGGS IN A HOT PAN AND HE WAS LOOKING HAPPY, AS HE
HAD HIS LOVE BACK INTO HIS LIFE.
CATHY WAS IN THE BEDROOM WEARING HER BLACK SKIRT AND RED
V-NECK TOP WITH BLACK HIGH HEEL SHOES ON, SHE HAD HER
SMALL BLACK SUITCASE READY TO GO.
CATHY TAKES HER SUITCASE OUT OF THE BEDROOM AND SHE TAKES
IT DOWN THE STAIRS, SHE GOES NEAR THE FRONT DOOR LOOKING
STRESS AND SHE TAKES A SIGH.
CATHY WALKS TO THE KITCHEN WHERE SHE SEES DAVID MAKING
BREAKFAST AND THEY BOTH LOOK AT EACH OTHER.
DAVID SAYS TO CATHY "HEY BABY."
CATHY SAYS "I'M GOING HOME."
DAVID SAY "BUT I'M MAKING YOU BREAKFAST. STAY FOR A
LITTLE WHILE."
CATHY SAYS "SORRY I CAN'T. I HAVE TO GO."
DAVID SAYS "WHY ARE YOU IN A RUSH TO GO."
CATHY SAYS "BECAUSE I DON'T LOVE YOU. LAST NIGHT WAS A
MISTAKE."
CATHY TURNS AROUND AND SHE LEAVES THE KITCHEN AND SHE GOES

TO THE FRONT DOOR TO GET HER SUITCASE, DAVID WAS IN THE KITCHEN STANDING THERE, HEARTBROKEN LEAVING THE TOAST BURNING IN THE TOASTER.

CATHY WAS OUTSIDE DAVID'S HOUSE WITH HER SUITCASE AND SHE WALKS INTO THE STREET, IT SOON BECOMES GREY AND CLOUDY IT STARTS TO RAIN AS SHE WAS WALKING DOWN THE STREET.

DAVID WAS OUTSIDE HIS HOUSE AND HE SEES CATHY WALKING DOWN THE STREET WITH HER SUITCASE, HE QUICKLY RUNS UP TO HER TO GET SOME ANSWERS FROM THERE BROKEN LOVE.

DAVID SAYS "CATHY."

CATHY STOPS WALKING AND DAVID STANDS IN FRONT OF HER, NOT LETTING HER GO AND HE WAS UPSET AND HE SAYS TO HER "I LOVE YOU. I WANT TO MARRY YOU."

CATHY SAYS "I DON'T WANT TO BE WITH YOU. I'M SAYING GOODBYE TO YOU."

DAVID SAYS "SO THAT'S IT. FINE. GOODBYE CATHY."

DAVID LETS CATHY WALK PASS HIM AND HE WALKS TO HIS HOUSE WITH ANGER AND HURT, HE HAD HIS HEAD HELD DOWN AS IT STARTS TO RAIN.

AS CATHY WAS WALKING IN THE STREET WITH HER SUITCASE SHE WAS CRYING FOR BREAKING DAVID'S HEART, IT WAS LIKE THE HEAVENS WERE UPSET WITH HER FOR MAKING A MISTAKE.

DAVID WAS OUTSIDE HIS HOUSE AND HE OPENS THE FRONT DOOR AND HE WALKS IN FEELING COLD AND WET, HE SHUTS THE DOOR AND HE SITS ON THE FLOOR FEELING WEAK, IT WAS LIKE HIS HEART HAD BEEN RIPPED APART BY CATHY AND HE CRIES.

COULD THIS BE THE END OF DAVID AND CATHY'S FUTURE TOGETHER?

OR WILL THE TWO HAVE A CHANGE OF HEART?

## Chapter Twelve
## Never Say Goodbye

As the months were passing by in San Francisco Cathy was back to her old self looking sad, dull and miserable. Even though Cathy did have a chance to be with the one she loved, she had her reasons not to be with David. Cathy was in the park sat on the grass eating a green apple; she sees an old seventy-year-old couple walking together holding hands, as they both went to sit on the bench.

Cathy sits there on the grass she felt trapped and lonely, as she was yearning for love and happiness but she had left it too late in her life.

Will Cathy visit David and ask forgiveness?

Cathy was at the embankment and she was sat on the bench like a loner, it was like she was waiting for something good to happen in her life, but that was not going to happen for her she takes a deep sigh of sadness and regret.

Later that evening Cathy was at home and she was upstairs in her bedroom, lying on the bed thinking long and hard about her miserable life, Susan walks in and she looks at her and she says "Are you alright?"

Cathy says "I'm fine mum."

Susan says "Are you coming down to have tea."

Cathy says "I'll be there in five minutes."

SUSAN SAYS "OK."

SUSAN WALKS OUT OF CATHY'S ROOM AND SHE GOES DOWNSTAIRS AS HER DAUGHTER, WAS LYING ON THE BED UPSET SHE DOESN'T BOTHER GOING DOWNSTAIRS AND SHE GOES TO SLEEP.

MATTHEW AND SUSAN WERE BOTH SAT AT THE DINNER TABLE WAITING FOR CATHY, BUT THEY BOTH KNEW THAT SHE WASN'T COMING DOWN TO TALK TO THEM.

MATTHEW SAYS TO SUSAN "IT'S BEEN TWO YEARS AND CATHY HASN'T SPOKEN TO US, SHE DOESN'T EVEN SIT WITH US."

SUSAN SAYS "DON'T WORRY GIVE HER TIME."

MATTHEW SAYS "HOW MUCH TIME. FIVE YEARS, TEN YEARS, FIFTEEN."

SUSAN SAYS "IT WON'T COME TO THAT."

MATTHEW KNEW CATHY HAD SHUT HER PARENTS AWAY FROM HER LIFE AND HE DECIDES WHAT TO DO.

MATTHEW SAYS TO SUSAN "WE BOTH HAVE TO DECIDE ABOUT OUR DAUGHTER, AND IT WILL BE THE BEST CHOICE WE DO."

SUSAN WAS SCARED AND WORRIED OF WHAT MATTHEW'S PLAN WAS FOR THEIR DAUGHTER.

WILL IT BE AN ARRANGE MARRIAGE FOR CATHY?

THE NEXT MORNING MATTHEW AND SUSAN HAD BOTH CAME TO A DECISION ABOUT CATHY, THEY KNEW IT WOULD BE THE BEST FOR THE THREE OF THEM TO MOVE ON WITH THEIR LIVES.

CATHY WAS AT HOME AND SHE WAS READY TO GO TO COLLEGE AND SHE WAS IN THE LOUNGE, TO PICK UP HER BLUE PLASTIC BOX WHICH HAD FOURTEEN EXERCISE BOOKS IN, WHEN SHE SEES HER PARENTS BOTH SAT ON THE SOFA, NEXT TO EACH OTHER LOOKING STRESSED AND ANXIOUS.

CATHY WANTED TO KNOW WHAT WAS WRONG WITH HER PARENTS AND

She says to them "What's wrong?"

Susan says to Cathy "We need to tell you something."

Matthew says to Cathy "We don't want you as our daughter anymore."

Cathy was horrified and she was trying to be strong about her parent's rejection, but her life had been shattered to pieces, it was like someone had stabbed her in the back and left her to die. She couldn't understand why her life was turning grey and ugly.

Susan says to Cathy "I'm sorry but you pushed me and your father away from your life."

Matthew says to Cathy "We want you out of our lives for good. We can't carry on living with your problems."

Cathy had tears flowing down from her cheeks, it was like her heart and soul had never existed, she turns around and she runs upstairs, she goes in her room and shuts the door, she takes a mournful cry as she goes to sit on the bed.

Susan and Matthew were both in the lounge sat on the sofa upset, they could hear there daughter crying and it caused, them a lot of pain and sadness to have broken Cathy's heart.

Saying goodbye to someone close to you is hard and difficult to cope with.

In life people in their lives sometimes have to say goodbye and they have there reasons, but sometimes it is not the best way.

A week later Cathy was at the embankment sat on the bench and she had her head held down as she had tears flowing down from her face, she did not want no one to see her

EMOTIONS.

CATHY WAS LIVING IN A ONE-BEDROOM APARTMENT IN TOWN AND IT WAS NOT FAR FROM COLLEGE.

CATHY WAS AT HER APARTMENT AND SHE WAS OUTSIDE THE TERRACE LOOKING UP AT THE NIGHT SKY, SHE THEN LOOKS DOWN AND CRIES, AS SHE WOULD SPEND HER LONELY LIFE ALONE.

A HEART WAS CRYING AND YEARNING FOR THE LIFE IT HAD. TINA, DAVID, SUSAN AND MATTHEW WERE OUT OF CATHY'S LIFE FOR GOOD.

IN THE DAYS, MONTHS AND YEARS CATHY WOULD BE GRIEVING FOR HER HUSBAND AND HER DEAR FRIEND TINA.

CATHY COULD NEVER UNDERSTAND WHAT LOVE MEANT IN HER LIFE, SHE WOULD NEVER HAVE IT IN HER HEART UNTIL THE DAY SHE DIED.